T0084457

LIGHT WITHOUT HEAT

LIGHT WITHOUT HEAT

stories

Matthew Kirkpatrick

FC2
TUSCALOOSA

Copyright © 2012 by Matthew Kirkpatrick
The University of Alabama Press
Tuscaloosa, Alabama 35487-0380
All rights reserved
Manufactured in the United States of America

Typefaces: Granjon and Berthold Akzidenz Grotesk
Cover and interior design: Lou Robinson

The paper on which this book is printed meets the minimum requirements of American
National Standard for Information Sciences—Permanence of Paper for Printed Library
Materials, ANSI Z39.48–1984.

Library of Congress Cataloging-in-Publication Data

Kirkpatrick, Matthew, 1974–
  Light without heat : stories / Matthew Kirkpatrick.—1st ed.
    p. cm.
  ISBN 978-1-57366-166-9 (pbk. : alk. paper)—ISBN 978-1-57366-830-9 (electronic)
  I. Title.
  PS3611.I764L54 2012
  813'.6--dc23

For Mom and Dad

Contents

Different Distances   1

Instructions   13

Light Without   15

Pennsylvania   39

The Saddening   41

Crystal Castles   47

Pineal Gland   61

Throw Him in the Water   63

Nevada   77

The Celebrations   79

The Most Amazing Attic   93

The AuralSec Story, A Corporate History,
    Chapter 7: Our Dependable Grampy   97

Animal Attacks   113

Glossary   115

The Board Game Monopoly   123

The Sodding   141

Pastoral   143

Iceland   151

Some Kirkpatricks   153

Acknowledgments   175

LIGHT WITHOUT HEAT

Different Distances

Conceived in a canopy bed in the Waldorf overlooking the wet black street along Central Park at dawn Sunday morning after an exhibition of my father's artwork at the Grace Gallery downtown. Warhol was there. Everything sold. Even the charcoal sketches tucked in Dad's black portfolio. Fabulous. Cocaine piled on silver trays and cases of Dom and Mylar pillow balloons. Best night of their lives.

In the bathroom at a Denny's on the long drive home from Piscataway, NJ. Dad had a job interview to paint houses.

In a Red Roof Inn at the juncture of three major highways ribboning into different distances, each with catastrophic, traffic-stopping accidents miles away. Dad never painted. Painted the walls of our first apartment canary-yellow, dreaming of landscapes and latex splattered from a ladder onto an enormous canvas below.

In a tent behind a condemned Lutheran church in Pittsburgh on the way back from six straight Dead shows. He had visions.

On the living room floor on a school night while my grand-parents slept upstairs. It was their first date, my first experience of love.

It was the best night of their lives.

Born in the backseat of my father's Buick.

In the backseat of a taxi stuck in rush hour traffic. Stuck behind an accident. In two feet of snow.

In the backseat of a NJ Transit bus stuck in the Holland Tunnel, three weeks too soon.

In the lobby of a downtown hospital and named for my grandfather, dead in the war. For my Uncle, dead in the war. For Warhol.

In the backseat of my father's Merc. Olds. Cutlass.

Named for the war.

Drought.

Meteors destroy my grandfather's house in Fayetteville, Arkansas. We spend the summer rebuilding. At night Mom thumbs dusty letters sent to my deceased grandmother during the war. Hail dimple-dents the hood of my father's Cutlass.

Mom dreams Dad painting plums, painting over plaster cracks, painting an orchard.

Mom dreams the night sky. Dad paints meteors. Climbs the steep slate roof of somebody's beach house on Long Island and paints the brown shingles midnight blue.

Learning to walk.

A record April snowfall blankets the East Coast. My first childhood memory.

Falling from the top of basement stairs cutting forehead. Despite the blood, my parents decide I can tough it out.

Scars.

My father's Merc bursts into flames.

Dad painting all night, Mom walking me by the hand slowly upstairs at seven, putting me away for the night so she can get down with some low funk (thumping up through the floor from below) and a tall glass of rye while Dad splashes paint across canvases in the cold, wet basement.

Led Zeppelin, Clapton. The Who.

Dad in the mirror combing my wet hair back with the black comb from his breast pocket.

Eno, Bowie, Reed, Blondie. The Dead Boys.

The first of many conversations my father will have about lenses and mirrors. He drops a salad bowl on the kitchen floor and slashes open the palm of his right hand. Wraps the wound in an old plaid shirt and watches it fill with blood.

Donna Summer. The Bee Gees.

Dad falls down a narrow well in the backyard. Lost for a day, Mom discovers him in the old hole sobbing. After 58 hours, rescuers lift him alive from the well surrounded by flashing bulbs and microphones and cheers.

Kindergarten. Drawing devils with black and blue crayons and asked to stand in the trash can when I refuse to select another color from the crayon box.

Asking Mom for a baby brother.

Mom dropping ice cubes freshening the drinks.

Dad painting black holes.

Sent home with a note.

The smell of my father's black comb.

Dad douses the door of my elementary school with gasoline and lights it on fire. Somebody pulls the fire alarm and we're evacuated out the back door while firemen flood the building.

Warhol visits and Mom makes meatloaf.

Warhol calls and says he's going to visit but never does.

Liza Minnelli sends my parents a postcard from Japan. Dad shows it to me and tries to explain the joke, why she'd sent it: an enormous lobster, claws poised open above its head, menacing tourists on a Tokyo street corner. They can't figure out how Minnelli got their address. Pour themselves drinks and turn up the stereo.

The Go-Gos. Public Image Ltd. The Birthday Party.

First recollection: shooting at other neighbor kids with toy pistols.

Gallery fire destroys a year of Dad's work.

He never paints again.

This Heat.

Picked last for recess kickball. Hunger strike: hoard peanut butter sandwiches in locker. First fat lip. Shot twice in the stomach by classmate with a concealed pellet gun.

Dad phones bomb threats from area payphones to cancel school. Gives me tubes of paint and names them as he squeezes each onto a clean wooden palette: umber, ochre, sienna.

Titanium, cadmium.

Draws my fingers through each and pulls my hands across canvases carpeting the living room floor. Cleaning our hands together in the basement basin. Turpentine still burning my nose, we hang our paintings together, covering every black wall.

Dad phones Mom twice and hangs up.

Poised at the wheel of the Merc pointed toward the distant border. Telling me we're leaving. Telling me we're going home.

Drawing secret maps during recess. Composing elementary manifestos. Declaring daily skirmishes and minor wars.

Dad sulking in the basement, surrounded by nude models posed on pedestals with hot lights shining on them from the floor. With a wet brush in each hand, standing paralyzed in front of five white canvases. Mom getting down to Grand Funk upstairs while I sit in bed. White Russians in a tall glass. Black Russians.

Dad painting a portrait of my head on the naked body of a thin, elderly woman.

Little League.

Black bombs red on canvas stretched across the backyard.

The taste of Warhol meatloaf every Wednesday, a hard-boiled egg hidden in the middle.

Painting in the rain and drawing his fingers across his cheeks, streaks of umber and sienna like the war. Shouts through the rain at the lightning, at the house, at the puddles flooding the world.

In New York, Mom tells the story of how I was almost born in the backyard. Almost born in a taxicab. Almost born at the bottom of a forgotten well. Three weeks too soon.

Breakfast at Denny's Dad feeding me fries reading *Parade* wearing sunglasses inside.

Helicopter ride over the Falls.

Dad brings home a paper sack full of GI Joes, some headless and some with twisted, broken arms and the hands chewed off. None of the guns match. Wounded in the war.

Dad drawing maps on the back of Mom's old dresses, wearing headlamps around the house. Tunneling into City Hall, into the Water Authority, into Toys R Us.

Tunneling into the A&P for a loaf of bread, a dozen eggs.

Too old for toys.

Mom packs crafty care packages for prisoners: knitting needles, thick skeins, rubber cement, scissors, magazine stacks, glass beads, glue guns, gum. Packs love letters on handmade paper scented lavender to shine light into their lives. Light shines into their lives.

Vacation at the Cape: Dad and I fly a kite on a wet, black morning, the wind whipping the kite across the dark sky. Storm clouds on the horizon, lightning flaring, the gray ocean always falling away. Running barefoot through the frigid water and laughing when the kite takes a dive into the surf. When the string breaks, Dad in clam diggers goes in thigh-deep to save the ruined kite and I run after him, try to tackle him into the cold silver ocean, drag him down with me.

Martha B: the blond girl who sits in front of me in Reading class. She wears a sundress almost every day and I stare at her soft back, imagining constellations in her freckles.

Crystal R: the blond girl who sits in front of me in English class. She wears a sundress almost every day and I stare at her soft back, imagining constellations in her freckles.

Beautiful blond girl in math class in a sundress, constellations across her back.

Buy a paper sack full of cigarettes and smoke five Marlboros in the school parking lot. I am in love with the cigarette butts arced around me on the black asphalt.

Parents divorcing. Dad telling me Nico from the Velvet Underground fell off of her bicycle in Spain and died.

Dad drunk paints the walls blue and pours red paint like a rug on the floor beneath the dining room table. Says he will never die.

High on glue.

Chess club, Archery, Student Council, School Newspaper, Bird Watching.

Softball, football, basketball, swimming, track.

Ski club, skateboarding.

Fishing.

High on cough syrup sitting in the cemetery.

Parents divorcing. Dad telling me Stiv Bators from the Dead Boys was hit by a bus in France and died.

Losing virginity in back of Dad's LeSabre.

Sent into the world.

Major in Film. In Journalism. In Agriculture. Major in Riflery.

Binge drinking.

Meet Sandy G the girl of my dreams at the pistol range blasting black stars into paper targets.

Dad starts painting lessons after painting houses for years. Fills the house with green mountain landscapes and frozen lakes. Mom leaves for a month, checks herself into some place.

Dad opening manhole covers longing for darkness.

Her neck smelling like gun powder.

Running over mailboxes with the Merc.

Her hands. Her arms wrapped.

Lighting fires on the neighbor's lawn.

Dad tunnels into the mall and paints wolves onto sweat-shirts at the Gap.

Major in

My parents dying in the Olds: black ice, tree stump, cliff. Dad electrocuted slicing through the orange extension cord connecting his circular saw to the house. Cutting wood for a canvas, a sculpture, a sandbox, a sieve through which he'll push the dry dirt in the backyard looking for something lost. Asleep in his bed one-hundred-years old.

Burned in a fire. Crushed in stadium collapse. Shrapnel.

Mom moving to Arizona to study with a spiritual healer.

A spaceship flying in the tail of Comet Hyakutake comes for them. Leaves their sneakers.

Dad tells me Mom fell from her bicycle in Spain and died.

Fall in love with Angela C making intricate books from twigs in the art department. Smoke cigarettes all night staring at stars on our backs on the golf course.

Dropping out of college with nine credits to go. Working at chain bookstore five miles from campus. The books stop speaking.

Lower East Side. Carroll Gardens. Astoria. Hoboken. Jersey City. Skyscrapers a black comb obstructing the sky.

First job answering phones at a downtown punk club. Sit at a plywood desk with a growling dog at my feet. Answering phones at a book publisher midtown. Answering phones at a Chelsea medical publisher.

Answer phones. Live in a brown box on a mattress on the floor. When it rains, my ceiling sieves brown water onto my bare chest, soaks deep into the damp mattress. Pray for the drowning death of all horrible things.

New Year's Eve: end of the century. The streets so full, we are chest to chest and sweat and hands. I lose my friends.

Wake in a ditch off highway 404 in Jersey City. Wake on a sidewalk on Avenue A. Avenue B. Fifth Avenue. Wake in my cold wet bed surrounded by the smell of mold. Wake warm in the arms of someone who will fall in love with me if only: a job, clean clothes, better home-baked bread, cowboy boots.

Fall in love with the girl of

Eating pickles wrapped in wax paper, eel rolls, falafel dripping yogurt over our fingers, leftover fries on the floor drinking scotch, bourbon burning through paper cups, splitting a can of beer, a box of red wine, fortified wine.

Dinner at midnight a view of

The paint peeling from the ceiling falling like thick yellow snowflakes.

Rainy vacations: Pittsburgh, Detroit, Albany.

Mom telling me about the streak of light across the sky and how the earth looks like a blue marble from space.

Miami, Vancouver.

Married to the girl of my dreams. To a blue cubicle facing a wall. To my old face above the dining room table. To unread books. To Martha B, Crystal R, to a ring of cigarette butts on the ground. Married to the war.

Honeymoon.

In Spain. In Mexico. Iceland in February.

In the kitchen hiding a hard-boiled egg in the middle of a meat loaf.

In the break room, old meat spinning in the microwave.

Spending the day on a green hill above the Hudson watching sailboats and helicopters.

Watching sweat through sundresses in this heat, sleeping in the weeds, raking fingers through her hair, cutting coupons at the kitchen table, cutting cantaloupe for Sunday breakfast guests, raking dead leaves with Dad careful to avoid the piles of soil, piles of damp canvasses rolled and gray stacked beneath the apple tree, the sun, the freckles on her bare back the zodiac.

Best year of my life.

Promotion and a good chair in sight of

Cat. Dog. Bird. Argentina. Barbados. South Africa.

Waiting for a flight, for the bus, for a taxi home late with a bag full of black binders. Waiting for Mom to call, for Dad

at the emergency room his hands burned black from a brush
fire in the field behind the house, the place across the street,
a bonfire in the backyard, burning bramble, stiff brown canvases, the drought dry gazebo lighting the night sky, sparks
like comets.

For the next

New chair, new car, dreaming of water and kites and

Trip away from this place.

The girl of my dreams slips listless

Seattle, Los Angeles. Niagara Falls.

Wake in each others' arms, the air conditioning cold across
our

Painted glass.

Cooking breakfast the smell of bacon and biscuits baking
coffee brewing waking up

Naked the sheets thrown on the floor the air conditioner
out kicking me away my body too much heat

Dad sending me a thick envelope of Polaroids of paintings
he did not paint.

We begin to run in the mornings that summer but the

Trains seize in the airless tunnels.

The landlord downstairs dies.

Kites grounded in the brown grass at the park by the river.

The smell of her sweat.

Dad missing Mom checks the well. Dad at the golf course,
the cemetery. Dad singing slow songs walking along the highway out of town. In the backyard with the metal detector digging holes.

The smell of her three days gone.

Move to the country. South. Suburbs. Home. Mom's blasting Sabbath, Dad out back building an addition, a gazebo, a bonfire. Building a studio in the old garage clearing away Christmases and ladders and broken toys.

The bird is dead and the cat claws at my hands. Something escapes.

The smell of her asleep. Her neck. Hands.

Estrangement. Separation. Divorce. Girl of dreams.

Binge.

Will move into a bright, cold

Divorce from heat, divorce from

Photos overexposed, photos of families cropped from magazines, photos of snow falling in the park at night.

And I am on vacation from love.

Will fall down the stairs drunk with Dad and break collar bone.

Will break toe. Fall down a well.

Down a mountain. In love with the girl of

Will break a bowl of ripe red fruit. Will watch Mom guide Dad by his old trembling hand down black stairs to the empty basement freshly painted gray where I'll cradle thick glass shards.

We'll kneel. Gather the pieces and cut our fingers, laughing.

Instructions

1. Your veil yawl is necessary.
2. Kneed a neckerchief into a warm spouse.
3. Distraught, then ice, then heat. Balmy salve, a poultice.
4. Insert into tab C. Start with the nails.
5. Locate holes in the length of
6. Sand and all other parts of nailing down inside.
7. Before the bird.
8. YAWL your veil is required.
   1. Believe this.
   ii   To open wide, to utter
9. wearily, having a smaller jigger mast stepped abaft the rudder.
10. Aspire a tiny thing.
11. Wintering owls in the silent
    night aviary. Translucent dome.
    A falcon hoisted high on a pole.
12. Unspoiled ice.
13. Mouth wide open, expressing weariness, shattering a smaller
    behind the door.

14. Identify the middle of the night after
    the spectacular out of them. It is small,
    now under the night sky

             a. in the cold.

             b. Not to mention the sweetness
                of bird songs. Glue

             c. and nail domestic support.

15. This position will no longer exist, as the birds in May and
    stopped in May, the predator is not necessary to actually
    be in a position to launch attacks on the courts.

16. It is almost May.

Light Without

Heat. This is the story of

born beneath an unknown constellation the shape of a whale devouring three

Two nearly identical babies born at the same time on a hot August night. An orderly at the end of a twelve hour shift, angry and confused by unfair events earlier that day switches the identities of the children before heading home to a tall Pabst and stale corn chips and a sleeping lover curled on the couch glowing gray from a snowy television. He finishes his drink and leaves his lover in the light. Beneath the glass a trapped star sizzles against the screen.

He has switched three babies in two months. At first he felt guilty treating parents' children like items on shelves. Switching babies filled some hole deep inside giving the orderly small power over the fate of tiny lives, compelling him to keep doing it.

Princes formed from all of Leo, half of Pisces, half of

She stands in the white light of the 7-Eleven and chooses magazines, looking at her reflection in the window, a mirror, until headlights destroy her image. She walks the aisles among the candy and coffee and condoms with a stack of magazines held close to her chest. She smiles at the cashier, a toothy grin in his smock. She lifts a single finger and waves at him with it. His face reddens and he retreats into the back room.

Drops a magazine into her black bag. Lingers choosing a candy bar something caramel and returns the rest of the magazines.

Pays for the candy and walks out into the snow and dark.

At home he lies awake imagining the horror of the wrong babies with the wrong families. He thinks that guilt will keep him from falling asleep but imagines his hands extensions of fate that must keep switching babies. He must realign the mistakes of birth for these babies. He is doing these babies a favor. Before he can work this out, he is asleep, and remembers none of it when he awakens the next day. His hands.

She spreads out on the clean beige basement carpet and thumbs magazines, choosing photographs of white boats on crystal water from above, a mass of bicycles, faces like petals on a rooftop against green hills and city lights. She inhales each page, pushing her nose into the seam.

the Big Dipper, two stars in Orion's belt, and a new star born
whose light has not yet
reached the Earth.
Leads a Leo life while invisible threads tug gently from
The chocolate on her fingers a mess, she idly taps the touch lamp base switching on, brighter, brighter, black. She pushes a smear of chocolate into the finish and lifts the empty wrapper to her tongue to lick the last bit.

She feels best in dim light listening to her parents' footsteps in the kitchen above invisibly tapping their toes to different silent beats. Her parents are always moving away from one another, only circling into proximity by mistake. She imagines each footfall marks a point on a map hidden between the floor upstairs and the ceiling above her. One day she will climb a ladder and remove each tile from the dropped ceiling to reveal the concealed map of some undiscovered place, routes formed from the pattern of her parents' movement.

She presses her cheek into the carpet and inhales the Mountain Carpet Freshness. She removes the staples from *Glamour* and peels the leaves of the magazine apart, spreading them around her. She scans them into her computer, sitting cross-legged with her finger on her laptop, cropping and pasting herself into other lives. She prints the pages on glossy paper and reassembles the magazine, stapling the pages so perfectly, so practiced, that only she would notice the difference.

Pushes open a window and blows cigarette smoke outside.

unknown images the size of

the sky.

She returns the magazine to the convenience store, reversing her ritual.

Somewhere a memory. A whale devours three Princes, brothers, a tail

The other baby became a famous television baby, her stardom brief but bright. She maintained a career for some time by being known as that famous television baby.

The orderly arrives late and smokes four cigarettes on the hospital roof before beginning his evening of avoiding whatever it is that he is supposed to be doing, looking into the hazy night sky imagining whatever interesting thing concealed behind the persistent city light.

She is fabulous, joking about her B-list status going to B-list parties and acting bit-B parts based on achievements she cannot remember experiencing. She studies her television baby self. She replays the episodes where her character functions like set decoration, not integral to television conflict, but something beautiful like a fancy plant, rewrites in her mind the scenes between cuts in which her television parents must bathe her and wrap her in thick warm towels and sing her to sleep. Writes the scenes that take place after the show's cancellation: riding with her father to guitar lessons, eating French fries with friends on the deck on the last day of school, skipping school riding in her best friend's convertible up to Malibu to lie in the sun and read from a favorite book and flip through *Glamour*, trying out for the swim team. The episode where she is beautiful but no longer cute so her parents adopt a baby brother. Had the show not been cancelled and lasted another ten years, her adopted baby brother would become the ring-bearer at her wedding, a very special two-part episode.

The orderly fantasizes about taking a baby home in the backseat of his blue Subaru to his girlfriend who has become less of a girlfriend and more of a fixture. He finds her most nights on the couch counting down the days until she will muster the energy to leave him. She would love a little baby and him, he, the father. He sits in the nursery in the rocking chair surrounded by cooing and gurgling sewing bright buttons onto a white blanket with invisible thread.

the size of the sky, the light the tip of the

fin a billion years away.

This is the story of

falling in love with an invented celebrity in a magazine at 7-Eleven. Falling in love with a room full of new babies.

Falling in love with a glimpse of a girl,

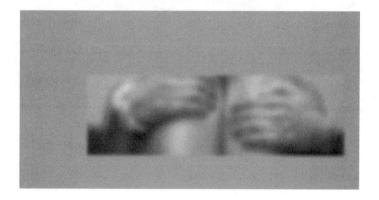

Falling in love with

Falling in love with

Walking across the park closed for the season covered by the first snow, sitting beneath a tree to have one more look at her in this cold fantasy, before returning to many fantasies all possibilities: a wife, a son, children, a dog, a cat, cats, daughters, an empty brown apartment, one black room above a cold bar, a private club where a Cuban soft ball team drinks and dances until dawn every Friday and Saturday, returning to sleep in his father's Olds, warm for the night.

Returning to a house and a wife and a son, returning to:

Returning to drink on the couch and watch the flickering light of the television until dawn. Returning to beige carpet. Returning to study stacks of video replaying them in slow motion looking for something concealed in fuzzy frozen frames. Returning to a hospital roof for one more smoke before returning to endless rows of babies in identical pink and blue caps.

This is the story of

Two women and a man, running across the field on the other side of the park passing a bottle, running by a man alone, sitting in a chair beneath a tree over the hill and out of site. He listens to their laughter. Two men, three women, one man running across the field on the other side of the park, passing a bottle, running by a man alone, sitting in a chair beneath a tree over the hill and out of site. He listens to their laughter.

Listens to

What he falls in love with is a room full of newborns, all possibilities.

What he falls in love with is a woman inserting herself into magazines, fingering a razor blade with her index finger carefully cutting around the heads of celebrities. A woman who special-orders glossy magazine paper, who un-steals magazines from the 7-Eleven, who inserts herself into other lives. What he falls in love with are legs, eyes, lips, hands in images not their own.

This is the story of putting one of the babies in a banana box at the end of the shift and throwing a coat over its sleeping body and walking with purpose into the hospital elevator careful to stand in the back between the gurney and two glazed nurses walking carefully out the back door and into the parking garage running up the stairs to the Subaru throwing the baby in the back situating the banana box between the spare tire and a dead battery to keep the baby safe for the ride home.

This is the story of running over a hill in the park at night through the cold, crisp snow, through a dark arbor to get to an aviary full of gray birds wintering. Running over the green hill past summering geese. Drinking from a bottle of Wild Turkey. Listening to captive owls. Noticing a man sitting in a chair in the snow beneath a tree reading a magazine on the first night of winter.

He curls the magazine and pushes it into his coat pocket and walks home to

something like a house and a family that sometimes he thinks is warm inside and fire and soft lights and plush things and staying up with his son asleep upstairs he and his wife watching a late movie and laughing, enjoying bowls of pretzels and popcorn and peanuts and Diet Pepsis leaving rings on magazines on the coffee table staying up way too late.

He stands in the empty kitchen, the sound of the new refrigerator full of food comforting him when he can no longer sleep.

He stands in the empty living room, his lover asleep in the bedroom, a sleeping baby in his arms.

At night when it is late and a nurse stands on the other end of the nursery drawing checkmarks into a checklist he will imagine all the babies crammed into baskets cooing in his bedroom he and his girlfriend smiling, overwhelmed by all the hungry things arranged so carefully in his newly blue apartment

Sometimes home is the desert.

The 7-Eleven employees are on to her but let her do it anyway because she returns the magazines and always buys a candy bar.

In the little room in the back they try to figure out why she would do what she does, flipping through *Stuff* and *People* wondering if they see her image among all the famous partying people. They carefully remove her pictures and hang them from string stretched wall to wall.

After checking the magazines she finds that all of her images have sold.

He buys every magazine he can find with her image.

In the kitchen at night he pulls his fingers across the granite and tries to remember if he ever touched the stained white counter they'd replaced, tracing his finger across black cracks.

A ball of yellow paper stuck between the counter and the stove twitches with the movements of a concealed insect. Something has stained the grout of the gray floor tile green. Sugar clogs the seam between the granite counter and backsplash, shining trapped in the clear caulk.

He tries to imagine the old cabinets and what they ate and stowed in plastic containers in the old refrigerator, not good enough. On leftover night he will admit that the new refrigerator somehow keeps things fresher. Or maybe it is the microwave.

The orderly's son: born under a dim star, born to be a baseball player, a guitar player, a horse trainer, a race car designer, a champion. He will wake his lover and put the baby into her arms and without words she will know everything the orderly ever hoped for or wanted.

In the morning at breakfast he will pour cold milk over his son's Life cereal and won't be able to focus on the boy's face. He will hear him crunching and be reassured that everything is as it should be with the boy's face.

His wife will smile as if she knows what's going on inside his head.

She cuts across the park at night because

She has lunch every Thursday and some Mondays at the Ivy. She shows too much breast, too much leg. She wears maternity clothes and too-tight jeans. She wears an orange tank top and no bra and golden skin and giant bedazzled sunglasses. She takes any celebrity that will go with her and makes out with them, sometimes without telling them she is going to make out with them. Sometimes they're into it. She orders expensive water and a cheeseburger rare cut into four sections.

She takes her television father with her and they make out. She feeds him a sandwich square for the cameras while he reaches for her left breast. He has a bit of something on his smiling lips. The photo will make it into several of the better smaller celebrity magazines and become an Internet fixture.

Something about his lips. Something about making out with her television father, an image of a real father idealized.

The orderly wraps the baby in the white-buttoned blanket he made in the rocking chair in the nursery and walks into the bedroom, red light from the neon sign hanging above the bar below glowing over them.

She wears disguises designed to make her look like she is somebody more famous. She dances around tables on the way to the restroom hoping to be caught in the background of some more interesting lunch caught on somebody's camera phone. She kisses people on their cheeks and steals French fries. She doesn't want to appear desperate, but that is part of her B-list shtick and she would like to be able to afford to keep eating lunches where people will see her. She thinks she will make a good reality series.

new light touches first cold clear space
something erupts

She pushes her hands into her coat pocket against the cold and walks faster when she sees three bodies running down the hill toward her. She turns toward a park entrance, toward the road, toward street lamps. It's too late for people in the park even though the light from streetlights reflecting from the fresh snow makes it feel like dawn.

She is between agents.

He dreams of a better microwave, dreams of a daughter, an apartment above a bar, another son, late nights out, another wife, a basement covered in dark purple carpet (on the walls, too) with a pool table, pinball machines, an exotic cat, a wet-bar. Dreams of.

Something above the ceiling of the sky.

The drunks catch up to her and say hey would you like some Wild Turkey. She's not old enough for Wild Turkey, but turns around anyway and sees two men and a woman bundled and red. They offer her the bottle and say hey you look just like that famous baby television star. The one from that show with the baby that was on years ago. I saw her in *People* and she looks just like you. This flatters her, so she takes a drink from the bottle heavy in her hand.

She has been waiting to be recognized.

The Wild Turkey burns her throat and tastes like something her father would drink when he is up too late and can't sleep standing in the kitchen pacing. She holds the bottle for a moment and takes another long drink mostly to prove to these people that this is not the first time she's had something to drink. The bourbon falls around her lips, down her neck, and onto the cotton collar of her red t-shirt.

He sits in silence on the edge of the bed until she stirs. He's unable to discern the details of her face as she sees the baby in his arms wrapped in a bundle of blankets. I'm leaving she says. He shows her the baby. Not again she says. The baby begins to cry and the orderly realizes that he'd forgotten to stop at the store. He puts his finger in the baby's mouth and this, for now, comforts him.

He sits in silence at meals increasingly unable to discern the details of his son's face. He has no problem with other faces. His wife still looks the same to him, but his son he cannot recognize, not because he doesn't recognize his son, but because he is physically unable to recognize the features on his son's face. He is a blurred photograph. When this started, he doesn't know.

Come back to our house and have a drink, it's not far. He offers her his hand and when she hesitates he steps beside her and slides his fingers into hers. The cold edges of his sweater are cold on her wrist, but his fingers are warm.

She is cautious because she is feeling drunk but also not cautious because she is feeling drunk. Television baby, come back with us. She melts a bit when they call her television baby so takes another drink when he offers her the bottle and follows them across the snowy park, taking slow big steps through the new snow.

Something like the light of a new star about to puncture the winter sky.

She follows paparazzi following better celebrities in her little car, parks where they park and follows behind. She stands in the 7-Eleven flipping through magazines wanting to be recognized, wanting to see her face among the A-list stars. She winces with each flash bulb flashing behind her, the photographers taking photographs of somebody more famous hiding behind their raincoat. She buys a candy bar and a copy of *People*, walking between the photographers perched in a row and whoever it is they are trying to photograph climbing into the driver's seat of a blue BMW.

Ruined constellations.

The drunks clear cans from the top of the turntable, put on a record, drop the needle, and turn it up. One of the drunks is cute, she thinks. He's wearing a red knit cap and a too-small flannel shirt tight over the tiny mound of his round belly. He switches off the lights and pushes the chairs out of the way into the crowded kitchen. He and another drunk carefully remove

the coffee table covered in tattered books and bottles and a stack of magazines into which she has inserted her image. They begin to dance moving their hips slowly to the small beats pushing out of the speakers. The other drunks drag something like a vacuum cleaner into the room and flip a switch and the room fills with fog. They turn on red and green lights and a slow strobe and begin to grind against one another in the way that drunks grind against one another in fog and light.

He sits on a stool in the dim kitchen and flips through his magazine, pushing his finger along her pasted-in page, touching her soft paper skin.

The cute drunk takes her hand and they dance, letting the fog obscure first their feet and legs, then their bodies and arms and hands and finally their faces are thick smudges through the smoke. The fog smells like maple syrup. The music from the tiny speakers distorts as one of the drunks twists the volume

knob. The wood floor is slick with a spilled beer. It begins to snow outside, the shadows of the slow flakes on the thin white window blinds. They will dance, they will kiss, they will kiss sitting in the park, their hands

His hands are cold.

Where have you been hiding, famous baby?

He hears thumping from outside somewhere down the street.

He sits on the edge of the bed trying to quiet the baby while she puts on her pants. I'll come back for my things.

The photographers feel violated and they laugh because they are violators. If she can't be in their photographs, she will ruin their photographs.

The room is so filled with fog and the smell of bourbon. They are arms and hands and fingers and lips and legs and light still in the flashes from the strobe.

He walks outside to identify the midnight thumping. He is small, tonight, beneath the cold sky.

He will return the baby before his next shift.

One of the annoyed photographers is less annoyed and begins to indulge her taking photographs of her behind the A-list stars because she is beautiful and sad and wearing these insane costumes.

He follows the noise down the block, the thumping becoming more significant as he walks.

In the nursery he will trade the baby for another baby and sit and knit and his lover will have come back and be in bed or on the couch or downstairs drinking in the bar.

But for a moment he holds the thing, waiting for it to stop crying, wrapping the blanket tight around its little baby body. Waiting for

(a photograph)

He asks her if she would like to go dancing some time and takes her photograph. She smiles.

She pulls a hand from her waist, pushes a face from her neck.

He knocks on the door trying to thump against the thumping rhythm so somebody will hear him.

They go dancing and he takes her picture dancing and feels self-conscious doing it because they are on a date, but she smiles and flings her head back like she is the most beautiful famous person. After the dancing they drive back to her apartment and she pours them new drinks and turns on the stereo and asks him if he'd like to keep dancing.

He takes a photograph of her dancing. She takes his camera in her hands and takes his picture. She turns him so that she can see both of them in the mirror on the wall. He is shorter than her, his jeans dirt-stained hanging low on his waist, his sneakers old and untied.

He comes close to her and takes the camera and kisses her taking her picture with his arm extended to capture them both. He lifts the edge of her t-shirt and touches her waist. His hands are cold.

When nobody answers he pushes open the door. Fog rolls out like water onto the front porch.

She pulls his hand onto her ribs and he takes another picture. He takes her picture, moving his finger along her ribcage, kissing her neck. He takes her picture. She will see these images in the back of a magazine, in the front of a magazine, featured in a magazine. She will see his thin lips on her face, see his fingers on her ribs. She imagines captions. She has become. She will be. She will never. She feels him moving his hand beneath her breast. A photograph is light. He takes her picture.

He stands in the doorway waiting to be noticed, waiting to tell them to turn it down. In the clearing fog he can see two men and a woman and a girl he imagines sits alone in her room at night her parents unaware of her cutting her legs, cutting her hands, cutting her face into other lives. He might tell her he is her father and take her home, rescue her from the light and fog and shitty music thrusting through blown speakers.

She takes his camera and lifts it high above her head and takes their picture. He begins to remove her shirt and she gives the camera a toss. The camera cracks the mirror on the wall and falls to the floor.

Don't go. You look just like that famous baby. The cute drunk shows her: the famous baby sees herself in the magazines as the fog drains through the front door. She is a B-list child star.

Standing over the babies in the dark he'll take a photograph of the baby and add it to the others hanging from a string stretched wall to wall in the little room in the back of his apartment.

She will ruin cameras.

She turns up the music.

He will kiss his son.

She lets him kiss her.

Light from a new star breaks through the darkness. One constellation is ruined, but new ones take its place. He takes her home. This is

(a photograph)

Pennsylvania

Valley. Minor mountains. Houses. Highway. Railroad. Dogs. Drunks. Litter. Grass. A Lattice. Aluminum. Milky-way. Shutters. Shrubs. Shellac. Swing set. Trampoline. Broken windows. Constellations. Rust. Basement. Staircase. Fingers. Hands. Arms. Unpainted bodies. Figurines. Ghosts. Scattered. Shining light into shadows. The tips of her fingers. Cold on the cold floor. Nestled in the dust. The tips of her fingers. Something glass. Sharp. Perfect red. A hidden array. A silhouette. A room. A broken lamp. A window. An empty swimming pool. A barking dog. A hole in a tree. A lattice of power lines limp, hanging black across the sky. Smoke. This dark land. A mountain.

The Saddening

Champion sat on the edge of the prostitute's bed and listened to the sound of her saddening. He liked to watch the prelude, especially; liked to watch her red lips quiver and her eyelids so tightly closed. The silence, too, of the room, so soft and warm, helped him to focus.

"Cry for the children and their mother and the dog that died in the fire."

She sobbed a little sob. Champion leaned forward in expectation. She opened her eyes, now red, but not wet with tears.

"Give me a minute, okay?" She closed her eyes again and showed him her clenched fists. She was trying.

Champion appreciated the effort and awaited her constipated tears. He leaned forward in anticipation of authentic sadness. His feet only in brown dress socks, his shoes untied and next to one another at the edge of the bed in the deep piles of the burgundy carpet, he felt only here warm. One reason he so often visited was for his cold feet and the softness of the bed, with her in her bra and jeans, her bare feet, her unpainted toenails, her eyes fogged with deliberate tears.

"Cry for me for all those babies in that bus. Think of them bouncing around in there, flying through the windows and screaming as the bus falls off the cliff into the icy waters below."

"What?" She opened her eyes. "That didn't happen."

"Please. I'm paying for this. It's happening right now in my mind."

"Bullshit," she whispered. She closed her eyes and wondered for the third time that day what had happened to the fucking. Most of her customers had stopped paying her to fuck them, instead asking her to perform various acts of what she had come to think of as emotional pornography. Most of her customers asked for sadness, but some, like Champion asked for other emotions, too: laughter, anger (her favorite), fear, angst (the hardest), and her least favorite, and the most obnoxious request, despair. She had long suspected her clients no longer felt anything for themselves.

Plentiful tears streaked her cheeks and, lucky for Champion who saw it as a sign of authentic sorrow, trickled over her lips and into her mouth, and so he relaxed. He sat with his back against the headboard, which felt loose to him. He would offer to fix it.

Champion would admit he used to enjoy fucking the prostitute, or trying to fuck the prostitute. Those fond memories contributed to his comfort in her apartment. More than the fucking, it was her portrayal of various emotions in the extreme that now gave him release. Release for him was intimately coupled with warmth, but also the clean décor of black, gray, the subtle splashes of dark red, the imitation mass-produced

Danish modern furniture, and the prostitute's stunning color photographs of wedding cakes.

At first, she thought the cakes might bother her downtown day clients, the good customers, she invited to her apartment, until they told her how much they liked them, how the cakes gave small pangs of something like feeling. Sometimes they told her they liked the photos because they made them feel guilty, or at least reminded them that they should feel guilty. Most of them complained the only thing they could feel was comfort, even though they wanted to feel other things, too. They often asked her to feel guilty and would confess things from their own lives so she could feel guilty for them. When she told them she didn't know how to portray a physical expression of guiltiness, that she was not an actress, really, they told her it was enough to tell them that she felt shame, or they asked her to switch to anger. That helped, too.

Champion was no different. He told her his assistant had killed himself and he had walked past the body floating in the fountain in front of the office for three days straight, ignoring the dead assistant, even leaving him voicemail messages and reporting him for unexcused absences even though he knew he was dead. In addition to knowing he should feel guilty for ignoring his dead assistant, he also felt he should feel guilty for reporting his assistant for bad behavior at work when he had a legitimate excuse for not getting his work done.

"I don't feel anything, really, except that I have to find a new assistant, and that bothers me, but on the other hand, Dale wasn't very good at much."

"I'm not your therapist."

"But then, a new assistant might be okay. I don't really care. I just don't want to have to fill out any paperwork. I don't want to attend any meetings, but I also don't want to have to go to sensitivity training. It's not like he was murdered. He killed himself."

"What do you do, anyway?"

"They sent me to the Gentle Hands facility for reorientation the last time something like this came up. That's what they called it, but it was really just a lot of sitting around and holding each others' hands."

"Reorientation?"

"I'm working on a very important project. I can't tell you about it."

"That's fine. Your time's almost up. Do you want me to feel guilty for you?"

"Sure."

"I'm not sure what that looks like."

"Maybe a little like sadness, but also a little like despair."

"I can try that."

"Can you shake your fists at the ceiling like you're cursing an angry God?"

"Okay."

After a bit of sobbing, Champion asked her if she had time for a little anger. She looked at the clock and saw that his hour was up.

"Are you ever going to pay for fucking again?"

"I pay for fucking all the time."

"It's been months. I get worn out by the crying. It's dehy-
drating."

"Why do you do it then?"

"Because nobody pays for fucking anymore. I don't understand it."

"Can I have some tea?"

She stood and he followed her into the kitchen where she
turned on the burner under the teakettle. A fly flew around a
dirty saucepan on the edge of the sink. Coffee grounds dusted
the counter. Outside the sky darkened. Against the window,
thick balls of gray hail smacked against the glass.

"You need to be out of here in fifteen minutes. I have another
client coming."

He handed her an envelope from his inside jacket pocket.

"Maybe on Friday I can get an hour?"

"I'll let you know."

"Do you print these yourself?" He nodded at one of her
photographs.

"Nope. I wish the water would boil."

He watched her breasts and her beautiful body as she stood
waiting for the water to boil. He felt a rare movement in his
penis and wanted suddenly to put his arms around her, bend
her over the counter, pull down her jeans, and fuck her in the
kitchen, and even though he was paying her as a prostitute,
something about this thought disgusted him after watching
her perform so many emotions over the weeks. It was as if they
had crossed some territory now that their passionate phase was
over and had entered a surer phase of subdued intimacy. He

didn't know how to go back even though, as he was thinking it, he remembered that all that was between them was a transaction. On Friday he would ask her to cry for him about the state of their relationship, the space between them, and the love they would never have. Maybe then he would ask her to have coffee with him, knowing she would refuse.

He stood behind her, close enough that a stray strand of her hair touched his cheek. He could put his arm around her and pull her toward him, but his time was up and instead of closing the space between them, he waited for water that would never boil.

Crystal Castles

Baby Jessica waddles across the autumn lawn. Cool gusts blow across the overgrown grass like thick waves of water. Pulled down by the undertow. Sucked into an old hole. Stretches her baby-fat arms across the circumference of the narrow forgotten well and hangs. Dangles feet above the cold earth below; dirt crumbling around her downy body down into darkness. Wind blowing through hair wisps. Cold soil around her waist. Something heavy dragging her down.

The Mole lounges horizontal on the couch in his subterranean living room thumbing the Atari control about to best his best Crystal Castles score. The lights flicker and the Atari resets.

Ever since being struck by lightning: She has no recollection of lightning.

Remembers playing in a tangle of
electrical cords behind the television and stereo pawing at plugs
like bristle blocks squished precari-
ously together. She would remember the stereo blasting something
adults called Journey and her parents on the couch rocking out with
Fritos falling from their mouths
and Pabsts. Remembers a dull jolt
like being punched in the chest and
smoke and an attempt at amateur
CPR despite her still beating heart.   Whiskers twitch.

What she remembers: waking up
in a bundle of blankets on the floor
her body and mind no longer bul-
bous and opaque, her childhood
cured by inadvertent amateur electroshock.

What he remembers is waking in
a bundle of blankets on the floor,
making coffee, eating a bowl of
dirt, checking out *Today* for a
while. After he figures out what
to do with the glasses resting on
his belly, he rummages around his
hole, finds poems unfinished in a
bundle beneath his pillow, a rad
Atari, dishes to do, and like many
of us pieces together from the shit
lying around his apartment what
he is supposed to do with his day.

When the darkness lightened and
her parents bent over her body say-
ing you were struck by lightning
something like lightning, she felt
something, blacked out and static,
hurt but bitter and wise.

Hanging above the well she
imagines the bottom full of better
Barbies and tea parties and worms
and a basket of batteries for all her
dead robot toys. She can feel herself
aging there at the rim, hear her
future in the darkness: first date,
middle school dances, and the cold
clawing and many marriages, to
images of an accident, being held
in front of cheering and cheering,
warmth, cameras, marriage to the
hole, marriage to an ex-con. She
will miss them all unconscious in
darknesses.

Like being struck by lightning
she does not remember the second lightning strike (drowned in
neighbor's pool) being hit by a car
(dropped) falling down stairs (hit
by car) burned in car accident (forgotten in backyard, struck by lightning.) Accidents somehow perfect.

Tired of hanging and trusting that
somebody will save her again and
enjoying the warmth radiating
from the well hole below her cold
feet she sighs and succumbs, sliding
down the narrow tunnel, her baby

This is a poem the mole wrote
about

Love:
The thing comes
of itself
Look up
to see
the cat & the squirrel,
the one
torn, a red thing,
& the other
somehow immaculate

Lonely Mole.

body toughened from so much
electrocution

roots and wire scrape her skin and
insect arms reaching out of the
darkness their claws clawing

at her newish skin
rot down here, decompose,
compost.

Throw olive pits and eggshells and
banana peels and coffee grounds
down on top of her and her body
will return to dirt. Let something
take root and grow in the decay.

Baby Jessica is surprised by the colors of dirt. Deep red, pink, black,
yellow like layers of birthday cakes.

Baby Jessica senses something in
the darkness in front of her.

The mole gags at worms so eats
dirt sandwiches, dirt with fries,
dirt spread over toast with straw-
berry jelly, hot dirt, cold dirt. For
protein, he eats dirt. This makes
cleaning dishes easy. The mole eats
a bowl of dirt ignoring his twitching whiskers.

When The Mole moved in he
painted the place red, pink, black,
yellow to remind him not to eat the
walls of his house.

The Mole can't ignore the whisker-
ing and investigates. He stands at
the edge of the old well and sniffs.

Floodlights from above fill the
dark hole. She hears them calling

Floodlights above fill the dark hole.
He hears them calling from above,

her name above, distant sounds
bouncing down the tunnel.

She sees a mole.
They stare at each other.

"Hello Mole."

"Where did you go?"

"Hello Mole."

"I'm Baby Jessica."
Baby Jessica is afraid to take

makes her nervous – no human has
ever extended a hand, never

fallen down a hole, lost and cold
she has
nobody but to trust

distant sounds bouncing down the
tunnel.

He sees a small girl.
They stare at each other.

The Mole is startled to hear such
a small girl speak, doesn't understand how she knows his name.
Frail and pale, smudges of black
across her almost white cheeks. She
shakes, from shock, perhaps – he
can't tell if she fell down the old
hole, or climbed down, though
her claws were very short so he
assumed a fall. Would she require
medical attention? How would the
Mole get her out of there? What of
the bright lights, the calling? What
does she eat?

He scurries back into his den and
turns off the television, then scurries to return.
"Hi little girl."
"I'm a mole."
The Mole extends
his hand
is cold and claws and fur and he
knows this
shaken his hand before, never
a talking Mole

never a beautiful baby girl

The Mole could help her, wrap her in blankets, feed her dirt. He has heard about little girls falling down wells before and knows that it could take days to rescue her – the danger of the well collapsing around her.

She finds the Mole handsome, debonair for an underground creature.

The lights above are bright and she can hear her name "Baby Jessica! Baby Jessica down in the well!"

The lights above are bright and he can hear her name "Baby Jessica! Baby Jessica down in the well!"

The Mole leads her and she lets him wrap a blanket around her and she takes the joystick in her hand. Despite knowing its function, she lacks the hand-eye coordination required for video games and loses on the first level.

He leads her into his den and wraps

A blanket around her. Offers her the Atari controller. "Crystal Castles!"

She loses on the first level and he's disappointed at her lack of hand-eye coordination. He's been practicing for years, though and doesn't hold it against her, puts the joystick on the coffee table and offers her a handful of dirt.

She thanks him for the dirt and doesn't know what to do with it.

He thinks maybe she doesn't know

She watches him eating the dirt
and believes that he intends for her
to eat it and she doesn't want to be
rude.

Are moles like birds dropping food
into the mouths of their young?
She opens her mouth and accepts
the chewed dirt and swallows with
as much enthusiasm as she can
muster.

She listens as he reads:
I dreamt last night
the fright was over, that
the dust came, and then water,
and women and men, together
again, and all was quiet
in the dim moon's light.

A paean of such patience—
laughing, laughing at me,
and the days extend over

what to do with dirt. He shows
her shoving dirt into his little
mole mouth and when she doesn't
understand he drops mouths of
wet dirt from his mouth into hers,
drops the mud onto her lips and
massages her necks so she can swal-
low.

He can tell she doesn't like the
taste of the dirt and is disappointed—he doesn't know what to
offer guests—he wraps the blanket
around her tight and reads a poem
to her: "This one is called 'For No
Clear Reason.' I am pretty sure I
wrote this one."

While he reads the Mole wonders
if he didn't actually write this one.
He can't remember writing any
of them, but each day intends to
write but plays Crystal Castles
all day – how else could he be so
good? He wakes up the next day
not remembering writing any poems, and yet with a stack of poems
scattered around his hole. Because
he can't remember anything, can't

the earth's great cover,
grass, trees, and flower-
ing season, for no clear reason.

remember reading, he assumes he
has written them, thinks maybe
he has written every word in every
book stacked in his den. Rewards
himself with a day of Crystal
Castles. Rarely with audience, he is
suddenly embarrassed that he may
be reading work not written by
the Mole and yet presented as the
Mole's own. He will begin to take
careful notes.

"That was beautiful, Mole."

He Blushes.

He gathers up the pile of papers
on the table and takes them to
the kitchen where he drops them
into the trash where tomorrow he
will find them and wonder why
he would throw out such precious
words and remove them and read
them and put them on the desk to
work on tomorrow after a game
of Crystal Castles and maybe a
little tea. He didn't write these, he
thinks. He means to write it down
on a post-it and put it on the refrigerator, and start some new poems
right away but hears Jessica in the
living room say

"Mole! I'm cold."

He packs newspaper beneath logs
in the fireplace and pushes her in
her chair closer to the fire.

A whistle whistles.

He wraps her in another blanket.

He puts a kettle for tea on the
stove.

He drops a teabag into a wide
ceramic mug and when the water
has cooled a bit he pours the water
slowly over the teabag and takes
her the steaming mug.
Too frail to lift the mug herself, he
holds

the mug to her lips. She sips, the
spice and citrus hot in her mouth
and

she begins to fall asleep. He pulls
a claw soft across her cheek and
sniffs her lips with his.

The next day the Mole wakes
and makes the usual discover-
ies—he has Crystal Castles! He
finds a stack of poems which he
assumes he has written in the trash
and wonders why he would have
thrown them away the day before.
He retrieves them and spreads
them out on the coffee table and
sits down to write but decides to try
his hand at Crystal Castles and sees

the girl curled up in front of the
fire and is startled.

"Good morning, Mole."

"Excuse me, little girl?"
"How do you know my name?"

"Remember me I'm Baby Jessica I
fell down the well and you found
me and read poems to me and fed
me dirt and made tea and kept me
warm?"

The Mole didn't remember, but
he decided it must be true because
Baby Jessica was beautiful and
sweet and curled on his couch.
He makes her tea and
he finds a can of soup that had
fallen years ago down the well and
she

she drinks another mug of tea and
eats the watery broth happy to have
something in her stomach besides
tea and dirt and he shows her

how to play Crystal Castles and
shows her the embroidery work he
keeps finding and together

she agrees that it's beautiful, lovely
work, so intricate. They wrap
themselves
the fire
above, the lights
they hear them shouting her name
bottom of a forgotten well
pressed together, their cheeks
hand

they wrap themselves and watch
hear the commotion
shining down on them like
spotlights, hear her name as if
they were listening at the end of a
cardboard tube their ears
pressed together their cheeks
in hand

Baby Jessica in the hole forty hours
with the mole creweling and cooking and eating and forgetting and
playing Crystal Castles together.

It's impossible he made it, he says,
without thumbs, even though it
is just that he doesn't remember
making it, usually before bed
he sits down to try his hand at
embroidery in imitation of the
beautiful pieces collected around
his apartment and finds that he is
really good at it, finishes a small
piece each night before succumbing
to sleep, waking in the morning
forgetting how it got there, redis-
covering his talent for needlecraft
and poems

The Mole considers asking Baby
Jessica to be his subterranean bride,
but can't help but feel like a pervert
for thinking about an eighteen
month old baby bride, but when
the Mole sits down to do the math,
he's got about 36 months total to
live and is now around 22 months
or so (he doesn't keep good track.)
So if the average adult lives to be
76 or so, then Baby Jessica is 38 in
Mole Years. The Mole, in human
years, is around 45. Acceptable
range.

Baby Jessica is rescued from the
den by claws that drill down

through the earth, widening the
eight-inch wide hole she had fallen
into. As she rises she looks down
at the sleeping Mole and longs for
him. As she enters the light of the
cameras and lookers-on she, too,
forgets.

She will become a photograph.

The Mole lounges horizontal on
the couch in his subterranean living
room thumbing the Atari control about to best his best Crystal
Castles score. The lights flicker and
the Atari resets.

This is a poem the mole wrote
about Love:
The thing comes
somehow immaculate

What he remembers is waking in
a bundle of blankets on the floor,
making coffee, eating a bowl of
dirt.

Cold in the hole the Mole looks
up, light shining into the well, and
imagines for a moment the glimpse
of a girl.

Baby Jessica will:

Say she remembers nothing, say
she has no recollection of falling
down the well and meeting a mole
and eating dirt and drinking tea
and falling down the well again
sixteen months later and meeting
a mole and eating dirt and drinking tea and falling down the well
again a year later, eating dirt and
meeting the mole and drinking tea
and sleeping in and playing Crystal
Castles and falling down the well
again, and again, and only when
she can no longer fall down the

What he will remember is waking in a bundle of blankets on the
floor, making coffee, eating a bowl
of dirt.

Cold in the hole the Mole will look
up, light shining into the well, and
imagine for a moment the glimpse
of

Pineal Gland

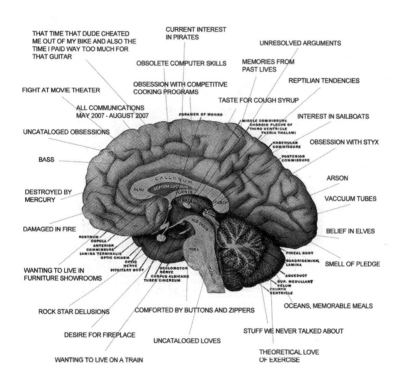

THAT TIME THAT DUDE CHEATED ME OUT OF MY BIKE AND ALSO THE TIME I PAID WAY TOO MUCH FOR THAT GUITAR

CURRENT INTEREST IN PIRATES

UNRESOLVED ARGUMENTS

OBSOLETE COMPUTER SKILLS

MEMORIES FROM PAST LIVES

REPTILIAN TENDENCIES

FIGHT AT MOVIE THEATER

OBSESSION WITH COMPETITIVE COOKING PROGRAMS

TASTE FOR COUGH SYRUP

ALL COMMUNICATIONS MAY 2007 - AUGUST 2007

INTEREST IN SAILBOATS

UNCATALOGED OBSESSIONS

OBSESSION WITH STYX

BASS

ARSON

DESTROYED BY MERCURY

VACCUUM TUBES

DAMAGED IN FIRE

BELIEF IN ELVES

SMELL OF PLEDGE

WANTING TO LIVE IN FURNITURE SHOWROOMS

OCEANS, MEMORABLE MEALS

ROCK STAR DELUSIONS

COMFORTED BY BUTTONS AND ZIPPERS

STUFF WE NEVER TALKED ABOUT

DESIRE FOR FIREPLACE

UNCATALOGED LOVES

THEORETICAL LOVE OF EXERCISE

WANTING TO LIVE ON A TRAIN

Throw Him in the Water

Mayor Whitaker treads water in the blue backyard pool, scissor-kicking beneath his big round belly, fluttering his arms in circles to stay afloat, waiting for his wife to call out the door to him.

The sky has turned red and purple and the warmth of the sun has gone and the skin on the Mayor's fingers and toes has wrinkled and shivers creep up his spine.

"Dinner's ready." He sees her in the window, her hand cupped around her mouth. She pauses and gathers her gray and black hair on top of her head and clamps it before closing the window.

Out of the water and up on deck he dabs dry with the soft beach towel Mrs. Whitaker put out for him. He wraps in it and flip-flops across the pool deck, down the pool ladder, and across the dead tufts of grass mowed down to the dirt, to the sliding glass door and into the house. Shut inside he seals the family from the quiet wind and the constant smell of coal burning beneath the ground all around them.

Inside it's baked chicken and green beans again and the kids circling the table like ornery rats. The Mayor drips. He takes off his turban bathing cap and sniffs. He tightens his towel and the kids look up at him, waiting for him to say the word. They've got their hands on their chairs and they're hungry.

Daniel, the oldest at twelve, is so close to a sneer, so close to "give me a break and let us sit down and have baked chicken for the hundredth time in a row." All the Mayor has to do is nod. Instead, he lifts his drink from the table, sloshes the cubes, takes a gulp and winces. He turns his back on them and flops away to change out of his swimming trunks.

They sigh and he smiles.

Janey and Warner watch Daniel work the lock on the fence. The combination's the Mayor's birthday. The Mayor and their mother are still in bed and the sunlight is already hot and bright. He's told them it's too dangerous to walk beyond the yard alone, that the fire's too hot right now and maybe in the fall. In the winter, it'll be safe, but when winter comes, he'll have some excuse then, too.

Daniel opens the gate and signals the others to stay back while he tests the road. What they worry about is the ground opening up beneath them so they're careful. His Adidas sink in the hot macadam. He pushes his toes further into the soft asphalt. It's not too bad.

"Be careful." He leads them onto the road. Daniel knows it's dangerous, but they need to do it, and they won't be gone long. They have an hour, he thinks, before it's really hot, before the

Mayor or their mother wakes and sees them not in the yard. Janey and Warner follow carefully behind Daniel, dancing from foot to foot and giggling as they get used to the heat.

Where the sidewalk starts they can walk on concrete and get away from the soft tar. They pass vacant lots where the houses have burned down and a few that haven't look almost empty, but not quite. Daniel thinks he sees something behind a curtain, hears a door close or a window rattle even though the wind is quiet this morning.

When the Mayor and his mother argue, when the Mayor tries to tell her he's not the Mayor of nothing, that the houses are still homes and that people will move back once the fire stops, Daniel thinks his father knows there are others still here, too. They hide and sneak off to the next town to buy groceries when they can and they think that they're the Mayor, too. That's why nobody acknowledges the others—they all think they've got a claim to what's left of the town and when the fire's out and people come back and come out of hiding, they'll be in charge.

The coal veins beneath the town have been on fire for so long, ever since Daniel can remember. Nobody is sure how the fire started, only that it won't stop. For years, most people lived with it and worked around the smoke and soot and sink-holes. Finally, when the fire *still* burned after so much time had passed and nobody would pay for the expensive excavation required to put it out, the town emptied except for a few who stayed despite what everybody told them. That's when their father and the others became mayors.

They're all paranoid, like they have to hide, as if the National Guard or whoever wouldn't have extracted everyone if they'd wanted. Nobody cares about them. They're on their own.

At the school, smoke rises out of fissures in the playground. The heat burning their feet through the bottom of their shoes is one thing with which they've learned to live. This discomfort isn't dangerous—they shift in place or stand on the sides of their feet or go in the house if it's too hot.

A fissure splitting the ground beneath them is what they're afraid of. The frayed seam around the cuff of their jeans smoldering and catching, engulfing them. Falling into the hole without somebody to catch them, burning in the caverns of coal below. Only a thin crust keeps hell from consuming them.

Daniel tests each pole of the jungle gym for stability and hoists Janey into a swing and pushes, keeping an eye on Warner running in circles. He knows to stay away from the fissures but sometimes after they've been inside they have so much energy they run and run until they succumb to the heat. Warner spins, teetering in circles like a top.

"Watch it," Daniel says. "Careful."

Warner nods. Like an airplane, he extends his arms and leaps.

Janey puts her arms out, too, and Daniel pushes harder.

"You'll fly away," he says.

The Mayor wakes when the bedroom is too hot. Brutal summer. Mrs. Whitaker's already out of bed. He pulls up his swimming trunks and stretches his swim turban over his head, slides into his flip-flops, and snaps down the stairs for breakfast. Out the kitchen window, there's everybody: Daniel, Janey, and Warner sitting in a circle in the sand mound playing volcano with a bucket of water and a decent pile.

Before his morning swim, the Mayor walks down the hill beyond the pool to the shed and carries feed to the chicken coop. On the way, he stops to touch each of his children's heads.

"Hot one," he says. "Careful."

They nod like they know what he's talking about and they've been careful all morning, playing in the hot sand, on the hot ground, under the hot sun. They all need drinks of cold water, but the water's always warm because the heat in the ground surrounds the pipes and the Mayor is worried about the electricity and the freezer is packed with food even though the Mayor's in charge of supplies and goes gathering in town every week. Maybe after they've eaten some of it, he'll let them make ice.

When the Mayor's away in the next town, it's a field day and the kids run down the street while their mother looks the other way. At night, when the Mayor comes back, he's tired. His day becomes her night, and when they've eaten and he's gone for a swim and had a few bourbon and Cokes and come upstairs to lay across the bed and sleep the deepest sleep of the week, she tip-toes out to the hall and puts on the clothes she's hidden in the closet there: a slim, shimmering black dress and heels to put on once she's where she's going.

She walks barefoot down the stairs and waits in the kitchen, listening for the Mayor's sleeping sounds. When he grunts she knows it's safe to go outside.

At night, the heat is almost bearable. The road's soft surface gives when she walks, but not enough to be worried. She'd feel a sinkhole coming, she thinks. She risks a flashlight and follows the beam around cracks and holes, up onto the sidewalk until it's crumbled, down through a yard, the grass long and brown, around withered shrubs and dead trees.

She walks for blocks and when she gets close to where she's going she turns off her light and looks to make sure the Mayor's not following. She's not sure what he would do if he found out she was sneaking away.

On the steps of the boarded-up hardware store under a dim blue light, she puts on her heels. When she taps on the door three times it opens a sliver and the soft music inside spills into the hot night.

Women in their best dresses sit around wooden tables with their legs crossed sipping cold beers or stand at a bar made from barrels or slow dance in front of one another.

"June," somebody says, eyes almost closed and smiling. "Glad you could make it."

June. She rarely hears her name. She is Mom and Mrs. Whitaker and the Mayor's wife.

She sits on a folding chair next to a barrel and opens the cooler and finds a beer colder than anything. The things they've given up to live here with no end in sight. She holds the bottle to her cheek, twists off the cap, and puts the bottle to her lips for a long drink.

The others, they're all married to their own Mayors. At first they thought things would be fine. Something would be done about the fire and their husbands' delusions would be extinguished. They'd pack up the things they cared about and move to the next town over and gets jobs and the kids would go to school and they wouldn't have to raise their own chickens or go on suicide missions for groceries. They'd have real restaurants.

She wonders when it might be right to leave, when she can get the kids together and get out and find a new life in the next town, but she's afraid. He's her husband and their children's father and before all these things happened he was fine and she rarely thought about leaving him. What if he caught them?

She would wait. Maybe he would wake up some morning and the flames would be consuming the deck or the pool would be too hot and he'd decide it wasn't worth it. Maybe the house will get swallowed and they'll have to leave.

Something slow comes on the radio and June joins three of the women in their dresses and heels on the dance floor and sways with them. They smile and sip their drinks. As the night goes, the heat gets worse in the hardware store and the ice in the cooler melts. The beers warm.

They don't dare open the door or un-board the windows. Nobody wants the Mayors to be forced to confront the presence of the other Mayors. Nobody wants a war on top of all the smoke and melting roads, so they stand there with one another with the radio low and make do with room temperature refreshments. They've got the night to themselves.

At three, she takes off her shoes and sits and finishes another bottle. Most of the women have gone home except for a few who stay and dance. She carries her shoes in her hand because her feet are killing her and the heat will feel good for a change.

When she opens the door the warmth outside surprises her and when she walks into the air she sees why: the house across the street is ablaze, fire jumping out of the broken windows. She watches the walls blue and orange with the heat on her face and smoke burning her eyes. Another window shatters. It'll burn to the ground before morning and nobody will care.

Daniel watches his mother leave every Monday after the Mayor's been out for the day and knows he can use Tuesday morning for an expedition. At four he packs his backpack with his own jar of peanut butter he's made by stealing an empty jar and filling it with a few spoonfuls each day. He does the same with the other carefully inventoried foods: saltines, hard butterscotches, and dried apricots. It's a drill for when they've got enough to escape for good.

They'll eat breakfast on the road. They'll have hours. Their mother won't be home until dawn and won't check on them. She'll slide into bed and the Mayor's worn out and will sleep until nine.

He nudges the others but they're already awake. Janey flaps her arms and Warner kicks. Daniel helps them get downstairs without laughing or tripping and once safely outside, in the coolest part of the day, he runs out of the yard and up the street toward the fissures and the smoke billowing from manholes. They risk the sound of running for the thrill of it and leap over crevices, run through smoke and weave around abandoned cars and streetlamps, leapfrog over hydrants. Daniel makes it over an overturned mailbox. When they reach the edge of their little, empty town they slow down and catch their breath.

The edge is a jagged line where bulldozers have destroyed the road so nobody can come back. Underground below them is the fire line.

White wooden barricades that blocked the way have been knocked down and rolled to the side to make way for somebody's vehicle. The kids put their fingers on the line at the end of the road and giggling, Daniel shouts "go" and fires his finger into the air and off they run, across the dirt and rubble and the hottest part of the ground, the burning ring underneath surrounding them and their ghost town.

"Ouch, ouch, ouch," Janey says, holding back laughter.

"Last one there is a rotten egg," Daniel says and even though he's the biggest, he slows down, pretends to succumb to the heat, lets it drag him down, his arms touching the ground as he stomps in faux slow motion. Janey and Warner giggle across the finish line, where the road starts again, where the barriers stand upright and the pavement on the other side is cool and firm and freshly painted with parallel yellow lines.

"Rotten egg, rotten egg," Janey chants. Daniel acts hurt, puts his hands over his heart and mock-sulks.

The sky is barely blue. Plenty of time. The air is so cool, it's like they've stepped off of an airplane in some foreign land. The road is wet and the forest around them quiet and lush. They walk with interlocked arms until they can hear the highway ahead, then veer off into the woods on a path.

The path is a narrow line wide enough for their little feet to walk through the thick ferns. They trudge up the hill. The tall, thin trees cut the sunlight. It's enough for them just to be away from the heat and dry air and to not be afraid to walk.

At the top, Daniel looks at his watch and they stop at a circle of rocks they've arranged there and sit and look over the valley to the next town and watch the cars and the little people and the trucks on the highway.

Every week when they sit down and it's cool Daniel thinks maybe it's this week: maybe they don't need to go back. They'll stay in the woods and wait until their mother and the Mayor can't find them and then they'll go down into town and figure out what to do next. It's this part that frightens him. If he was old enough to get a job, if he knew somebody, if he could find the Gramma or Grampa they barely remember, he would do it. Maybe he can convince their mother to take them and if not, maybe next year when he's thirteen.

They unwrap their breakfasts and eat, pointing out to each other when they see something moving, alive down there.

When the Mayor wakes up on a Monday and it's time to go into town to do the shopping, he looks in the checkbook and sees how much money is left and mentally calculates how long they can stay there before they need to start collecting taxes. They've got the chickens in the back, and he'll try hunting in the fall. They'll be okay for a while, long enough for the people to come back and create some revenue. He'll pay himself a modest salary and get to work on improvements. He'll pave the roads, open the school, and have a victory celebration for everybody who's returned. He'll have a quiet moment and thank his family for their support in all this, for believing in him and their town. He'll cut a ribbon.

He walks to the edge of town, where the heat subsides and the rubble of the bulldozed road becomes a road again and walks down a dirt path to where he's hidden his small car, the red Chevette he found after the second round of evacuations. It takes a while for the car to start but once it does he is hell on wheels and floors the gas.

In town, he watches families walking past the old movie theater, now closed, the luncheonette, the barbershop, the pharmacy and thinks about all they could have if he'd just give up and move here. Find a job like he used to have. Buy a house. Get a real car.

He could never be Mayor here, and his kids would be crazy with all the distractions. At home they can play in the backyard and there's nothing to worry about. He's already asked them to sacrifice so much. They can't give up.

When the people come back to their own town, when the fire's subsided, he'll be in charge and they'll have all the friends they'll ever need and they'll have more opportunities than they ever could somewhere else. The fire is a blessing.

At the strip mall, he fills a cart at the Shop and Save with anything on sale. They've already got chickens from the chicken coop, potatoes from the potato patch, and herbs from Mrs. Whitaker's window box garden. He drags a twenty-pound bag of rice from the shelf and lifts it into the cart next to the cans of green beans. He knows this is overkill, that he oversupplies them, but he is never sure when the fire will lay siege.

On the way home, the Chevette chugs under the weight of rice and canned goods and boxes of snack cakes. He makes one last stop before getting on the highway: the Friday's right before the on-ramp. He sits at the bar where he can see the television from the high stool and orders a giant draft Miller Lite and holds it to his lips like a chalice and drinks, the beer running down the sides of his mouth, soaking his shirt collar. He watches the baseball game and they bring him his usual: the Appetizer Tower, three levels of glaze-soaked ribs, chicken bits, and tiny crispy shrimp all thick and sticky with extra sauce on the side.

He could get used to this life all the time but he knows it wouldn't be good for his family. He'd have to get a job, so no more swimming all-day and walking around in nothing but shorts and flip-flops. He'd have to give up his Mayoral dreams and face things, and right now, that's not an option.

They bring him a steak, rare, the biggest the chef can find, and after that, another beer, and after that, two pieces of chocolate cake. He eats the cake slowly, now; he's almost out of room and he dabs the bits of chocolate and left over glaze from his lips and cheeks and drains the last of his fourth enormous beer and when the baseball game is all but over he sits back and puts his hands on his belly and smiles, because he's the Mayor.

The Mayor backstrokes in circles around the pool and Mrs. Whitaker stirs rice inside and gets ready to slaughter another chicken, good for a dinner and a lunch. The kids are in the yard, pushing their trucks through the sand. The heat from the ground is unusual today. The air smells like somebody is cooking out even though it's probably a house on fire or a burning tree not far away. It's a deep heat, but because they play on the ground every day, they're used to it, and they let themselves get a little warm. Maybe they'll get in the pool with the Mayor, later, before dinner, and cool off with a few laps.

Mrs. Whitaker walks across the dirt yard, fed up in bare feet and smiles at the kids. Janey's deep in thought with her little metal bulldozer, digging a trench around an imaginary blazing town. They all know how to fix it. If somebody would spend the money they'd dig up the burning veins. It's legend now.

Mrs. Whitaker blows a kiss to her husband up in the pool, but his eyes are closed and he doesn't catch it. Down the hill in the coop, she grabs a good chicken by the neck and walks it out to where the others can't see, to where there is a block where she holds it down and picks up the hand ax and one, two, three, she chops off its head.

The other chickens in the coop screech like they know what's happening and she starts to walk back up the hill with the bloody ax in one hand and headless chicken in the other on the way to see her husband in the pool. She stops and considers what she might do with the ax and how, without the Mayor, things would be simpler. There are no police here, no neighbors. She could do it, gather the children, and walk right out of town and nobody would ever know. He'd float face down dead in the pool water and they'd be free.

What the children will think is the only thing that bothers her about it and it stops her. She looks down at the blood all over her dress and stops. She can't do it. She feels in her feet a rumble in the ground. The pool water ripples while the Mayor floats. The children's sand towers crumble.

When the earth fissures and swallows their sand and then Daniel, Janey and Warner grab him by his burning shirtsleeves and scream. A cloud of smoke and steam envelops them as they tug at Daniel scrambling to keep from falling into the hole. He's worried because he knows they can't hold him for long.

Daniel is their escape and even though they love him, this is what they think about. Who will take them to the playground? Who will take them to watch the next town over and lead them out when the time is right?

They'll pull him up from the crevice, drag him across the dead dirt lawn, struggle up the ladder and throw his burning body into the blue water and save him. Next week, when the Mayor's sleeping in, they'll get their peanut butter and anything else they can gather and cross the fire line into the cool dawn mist on the other side and never come back.

Nevada

A nuclear detonation was conducted below this spot at a depth of 3,200 feet and is hereby commemorated by eternal rust-cap. Note the weeds circling the perimeter. Note this toxic hole. Here explosives exploded. The ground fell feet into the ground. The device, with a yield of less than one megaton, was detonated to determine the environmental and structural effects that might be expected should subsequent higher yield underground nuclear tests be conducted in this vicinity.

No excavation, drilling, and/or removal of materials is permitted without US Government approval within a horizontal distance of 3,300 feet from the surface ground zero location (Nevada State Coordinates N1.414.340 and E29.000. Nye County, Nevada.) Do not open the cap for toxic inhalation, no matter how strong the urge. Imagine lavender, imagine odorless white radiation, imagine radiation radiating, the sun's rays up from this hole. Imagine always summer. Any reentry into US Government drill holes within this horizontal restricted area is prohibited.

The Celebrations

1.

- Tonight there's this, obviously.

- How do they get the fragrances so realistic? I can't even tell these are fake.

- They didn't give him the job. They said he was morally questionable.

- I wasn't going to.

- I think they're too tight.

- We're working on new jargon to sell to businesses.

- I'm not sure what that means.

- How do you know her?

- She tried to fuck him in the bathroom while his wife was asleep in the next room.

- I didn't know you wanted to go.

- I thought we'd be the only ones here.

- I was going to stay home and work on my creations.

- He designed their lightshow.

- I think she died in a fake fire.

- Sure, it's probably illegal.

- I don't know whose it is. It seems angry.

- They caught him looking at porn while he was waiting for the interview.

- Look at these.

- Oh, I think she had intended to tell him at some point, just not like this.

- I stepped in it again.

- They had him on camera.

- I think I've had enough.

- What we're doing is pitching countries with boring food. Dull cuisine.

- How did it happen? Some idiots think they're performance artists, then a bunch of people panic and get stuck in the revolving door.

- Taste this.

- Where did he go?

- Canada. We're targeting Canada. And some of the eastern Europeans. Belarus, Latvia, Estonia.

- Why are you being so weird?

- I think he was touching his dick through his pants.

- I don't understand.

- It adds a little baldness. It makes your hair recede. See? Don't I look older, more mature?

- I didn't know you wanted to go.

- Why are you so mean to me?

- She followed him in there. I don't know what he did. He can't be that stupid.

- Aren't you afraid you'll get caught?

- It's really only a matter of time before these things hit, I think. I'm really onto something.

- I didn't have anything better to do.

- I didn't know you wanted to go. You can come over now.

- What do you think it was?

- Is it that obvious?

- Narcissism? It's like nobody can connect with anyone else anymore because they're only into projecting how awesome they are. How else could he be so insecure?

- Not too much. Who made you?

- I should have worn it.

- Is somebody knocking?

- It's not that late.

- Did you taste this?

- I'd high-five his ass, too. But he's married.

- Have I introduced you to my lover?

- You're not making any sense. I'm making sense.

- He doesn't love her.

- I was stuck in traffic.

- It's never going to snow again.

- Where is that crying coming from?

- Here's an example. Have you ever heard somebody say is it bigger than a breadbox? Smaller than a car?

- Why didn't you just tell me you wanted to go. You can go.

- I like her breasts a lot.

- No, you've got it wrong. She was fucking both of their husbands. This is different.

- It's not that far from where you are.

- I would have worn my new dress if I'd known.
- Do you want to come over tonight and see it?
- Why would anybody want to buy that?
- My apartment's only a few blocks from here.
- He's doing it again. I swear.
- Why are there so many air filters in here?
- Why is it crying? I don't know how to make them stop.
- I don't really know how long it will last. It doesn't bother me that much.
- It's getting late.
- It's really cramped in here.
- I'm not sure how he thought he'd get away with it. I think he had his briefcase over his lap.
- And who, then? Tell me.
- We'll design them as little as a signature dish, or a menu, or we'll evaluate growing conditions, raw materials: how many eggs a year do they produce, for example.
- You're being weird.
- It's unbelievable.
- Does it look blue to you?
- I thought it was part of the interview.
- They make me uncomfortable.
- This wine is terrible.
- It's not really like blackness, just spaces of time that I don't remember. It's like I was asleep, but also not like that at all.
- Nobody else seems to be paying attention to it. I think we should just walk away.
- I don't go there anymore.

- Are they leaving together? He's just in the other room.

- The note said something about meeting her on the roof.

- He's in the chair in the corner. He just turned off the table lamp.

- She told me they die after a few days, even. Just like real ones, except a little brighter.

- We want to replace all those words with one word – bread-box. We're really talking about efficiency.

- Tell me your favorite. I like this one best, but they're all good, don't you think?

- I'm making my move.

- She's doing it again. Look at her hands. His wife's in the bathroom. Unbelievable.

- You made out with her. It's your own fault she kicked you.

- How many eggs *can* they produce in a year, that's what we're trying to figure out.

- We should have gone to a movie.

- I wrote them a letter. I told them I thought the area where they keep the milk is disgusting.

- Something about lips. I don't really know.

- Come on, don't back down now.

- Why aren't you talking to me?

- He ran off with his teacher.

- He works there. He tests them or something.

- Who brought a baby?

- She calls him her *lover*. Who says that?

- It's for young people. To make them look a little older.

- They sent some coupons.

- I know it seems strange, but trust me it's going to save a lot of time, and if you're saving time, you're saving money. We'll probably come up with a word for that phrase, too.

- Just move these coats. There's room.

- It's never quiet there.

- See how he's holding the pillow?

- Do I disgust you?

- Quite a bit older. I'm sure it's a phase.

- Well, one time I woke up in somebody's backyard, which seemed okay at first, only after walking lost around the neighborhood for a while I realized I was in Philadelphia.

- Do you think anybody saw us?

- Just stop. You're being an asshole.

- There's a fertilizer for it. They add it to their feed.

- Can I smoke here?

- I don't think she's wearing a bra.

- It's just a side effect. But seriously, I feel like a kid again.

- How does my ass look?

- There's something in it about people who fuck whales, or want to fuck them. I don't know if they actually go out and try to make moves on whales, or what they do. It might be dolphins.

- He brought home a whole case of them.

- What we do, is we monetize the edges of that curve.

- We're not going to get caught.

- I'm sick of this.

- Oh god, they're beautiful.

- I don't even know what real grapes taste like anymore.

- I don't know, I can't find him. I haven't seen him since we got here.

- I have to go to this performance. He choreographed the dancing parts, so I have to.

- How does it taste?

- Oh God.

- Why is he wearing a tracksuit?

- Can I touch them?

- I swear he's touching himself. Look at his hands.

- If you say breadbox, everybody knows you're asking about project scope. That's the idea, in a nutshell.

- I didn't have my wallet or anything.

- I was up on the roof getting some air.

- I don't know. Shouldn't somebody call the police?

- No, you're not getting it. A whole new cuisine. Take Canada, for example.

- I don't know. He told me he sold them. I don't know for how much.

- That's the beauty of it. Thicker shells. The yolks and whites stay the same, but they can charge more.

- I'm sure he'll come back.

- Why are you spending so much time over there?

- Please be quiet. Somebody will hear.

- I'd fuck him, I think.

- I know, I think he has a problem.

- I said 'good riddance' and then she told me he was dead.

- Is his hand up her skirt? In the open like that?

- Are you hot for her? I'm standing right here.

- Do you think it's safe to leave?

- Is he going to finish? It's disgusting.

- I don't have a problem. You're just an asshole.

- I think you can see my penis too much in these jeans.

- We're going to productize it.

- Have you ever seen something this color before?

- They found him naked in the aquarium.

- What we're hoping to do is reduce workplace conversations. Instead of having to go through the usual litany of questions, you just replace them with our jargon. Breadbox. Money time. Fired. See, it's easy. From there we'll move on to social situations.

- Maybe it's hungry.

- I'm sure it's terrible. Please don't tell him I said that.

- Not a big one, one of the smaller kinds.

- Would you like me to tell you about my project?

- I think it's lime.

- You're telling me you'd fuck him. He's beating off at a party.

- People don't really trust young people.

- It's not fair. I didn't know they would be watching.

- Is that wine?

- Oh, they're gay.

- Artificial fragrances, sure. Now we're working on discovering new colors.

- Do you want on this rocket, or what?

- One of us is just going to have to go for it.

- I feel a lot better now. I didn't want to go, but I'm glad they made me.

- Just ignore it. I'm sure they'll call the police when nobody's claimed it.

- I wanted to wear this dress, but I thought it was too much for something like this.

- I think he has his hand up her skirt. I think he's fingering her right there. In front of everybody.

- You're not getting it. If the yolks are bigger, they lay fewer eggs. That's the key.

- We didn't even come together.

- What were you doing in the closet?

- It's not our problem. We don't live here. Just walk away.

- I'll draw you a picture.

- Nothing natural is this color.

- I think she's trying to fuck him in the kitchen.

- I called my sister and she bought me a bus ticket.

- Do they know how disgusting that is?

- It makes the eggs bigger.

- I was in the kitchen.

- Money.

- Aren't we friends? I thought we were friends.

- Why'd I come up here with you?

- It'll take years before anybody notices.

- I'm not sure how we get off. We just ride it and see where it goes.

- No he's not. His hand's on her thigh.

- Only big projects. We might consider a city if they needed a signature dish. If Washington DC needed the equivalent of deep-dish pizza. Or we might help the Native Americans put together something marketable. A menu for a franchise, maybe.

- A lot of that time is taken up by darkness.

- Each hen can only produce so much yolk. The key is to spread it around more eggs while making the eggs heavier. Heavy eggs are money.

- It's just a metaphor.

- We think of it as a way to add synergy. We help the left hand know what the right hand's doing. We bridge gaps. We make molehills into mountains and then back again. That's what we do.

- I've been here the whole time.

- The problem is that you never talk to me anymore. Nobody sits and talks. We need to talk.

- When's the last time you ate in a Canadian restaurant?

- Why would anybody pay for that?

- I think it's hungry. Or something.

- Her husband's on the roof. I can't believe she's letting him do that to her.

- Why would I do it? They had porn magazines right there in the lobby. What was I supposed to do?

- I need to take this. Excuse me.

-Then we'll move on to family recipes. Set up a whole food story. Grandma's sweet potato pie. Auntie's sugar cookies. Dad's brats. Mom's meatloaf. We do it all, though: photos, mementos, memories.

- That's why I didn't invite you. You're being an asshole.

- I'll give you a card.

- Can I just get my jacket?

- Unbelievable.

- I wore it for you.

- Breadbox.

- I didn't know. I thought they'd gotten divorced.

- I think he's going for it. Right there in front of her.

- I don't know how to describe it. Just long periods where I don't remember anything.

- Where have you been?

- Why?

- We just walk away. Pretend we were never here. This never happened. That's how.

2.

The sound of laughter. The sound of shoes on broken glass. The sound of violins through a wall. The sound of howling through the thick window. The sound of distant spring thunder. The sound of whispering. The sound of low music. The sound of lips. The sound of rain seeping through the ceiling tiles landing in a bucket in the spare room. The sound of a key turning in a lock, the sound of a door closing. The light from a camera flash, the vibrating of cell phones, the smell of hair, the smell of something burned in the microwave, the smell of gin spilled across the bed, the smell of smoke from an extinguished flame. The smell of lemons. The smell of bodies. The feel of the tile floor through thick soles. The feel of breath on the lobe of an ear. The feel of a hand glancing another hand. A murmur, murmuring, murmurs. The draft from beneath the door.

3.

Forty-six feet and one inch separate the toe of a black leather shoe positioned at the border between the outside hallway and the inside of the condominium from an index finger resting on the metal railing of the balcony. The glass door between the balcony and the gathering room is open. A slight wind, warm. On the plane formed by the index finger, a sliver of skin between skirt and sweater edge, and the number five on the face of a watch, a triangle: 33°, 110°, 37°, 19 inches, 17 inches, 29 inches. A browning flower pinned to a jacket thrown across a chair, a framed photograph fallen behind a bookshelf, a missing glove. Eighteen feet, nine inches in a line from the index finger to a back pressed against the closed glass door separating the balcony from the bedroom, dark. The palms of hands pressed against glass. Eighteen feet, four inches from the wall separating the outside from the in, a piece of clear broken glass. Six feet, 30° from a line, parallel to the wall separating the gathering room and the balcony, formed by a black spot on a red rose in a white vase on a cherry stand against the yellow wall and the black spot on the opposite wall where a spider has been killed, a hand touches a hand. Mouths move. A moth flutters around candlelight. Five feet, four inches from the index finger on the balcony rail, through a closed glass door, in the bedroom, a hand moves. A door closes. Lights dim. Thirteen feet from the edge of clear glass hidden in the white carpet, a foot, a shadowed man in a chair. Forty-two square feet of standing room in the kitchen, the entrance thirteen feet, three inches from the glint of broken glass hidden in the carpet. Fourteen feet stand in the kitchen, each foot occupying approximately three square feet of space, depending on the shifting of bodies and laughter. Shifting angles on many moving planes. The lines between eyes and eyes and mouths. The heat of a hand. The heat of a face. The space between the edges of each tongue fluctuating. The angles of celebration.

The Most Amazing Attic

A striking kitchen just like the basement. Rummage the attic in your mind. A basement with or without a den. Discover the wonders of an omelet. A team of scientists under orders from a dictator reconstructs bread, socks, cafes, knives, and bicycles from DNA. Death is good. Succumb to expensive wine, cocaine, prostitutes, silk shirts, and massages. Go into debt. Moonlight and steal. Animals give you a fresh perspective on the lives of animals.

Some animals: fox, cat, rattlesnake, crow, coyote, clone, cowboy.

Play golf. Go to battle.

Collect the following: Stamps, famous friends, languages, mystical experiences, animals, toothbrushes, chocolate bars, mushrooms.

Visit a farm. Visit a field. Visit a pasture. Visit a construction site. Visit a war. Visit the ocean in a boat or a ship or swim or hang out on the beach and eat mushrooms. Visit a forest. Visit an animal. Visit a tree. Cut down a tree. Hunt. Eat whale blubber. Visit a hill. Visit a mountain. Visit a town. Visit a city. Visit a river. Visit a street. Visit a bench (when available.) Visit a stadium (any stadium will do.) Visit a cemetery. Visit a public swimming pool. Visit a city. Visit the courthouse. Visit the slums. Visit the suburbs. Perform surgery. Visit a party in progress. Perform miracles: meteorite shower, comet, forest fire, earthquake, nuclear explosion. Attend a football game in which a touchdown is made during a tornado.

Did she run away? Was she kidnapped? Are you responsible? How? What do you do next? Do you go on a nature adventure (raft trip, drowning, skiing)? Do you perform love-making? Do you dump the body at the dump, a construction site, a jail, a hospital? Is the moon gone? Are you on fire? Make it erotic, pointless sex. Do it at a construction site. Describe it blow by blow. Use food. Have a four-year-old watch.

A hunter is tempted to aim for one of the other hunters instead of the deer. This might be a good scene.

End up in jail. Talk with some liars. Talk with some truth tellers. Tell the truth tellers you think they are liars. Talk to some construction workers. Try to seduce the person you are talking to. Gossip. Be pretentious. Struggle with money and relationships. Argue with some immigrants. Converse with Satan. Visit Las Vegas or Club Med with Satan.

Have some dinner.

Record conversations.

Say something nutty.

Sit quietly and listen to the voices. What are they telling you to do? How quickly can you do it? Will it take you to a construction site?

Create anger, depression, love, hate, fear, longing, loathing, cynicism. You have an annoying, grating voice. Create clouds, wisps, smoke, seagulls. Find a nude model. Paint the nude. Give the nude a soul. Have some more dinner. Light a fire. Describe the tools at a construction site: hammer, gun, thermometer, rope, syringe. Feel the sensation of your skin. Describe the subway. Evoke smells. Kiss your aunt in an unusual way. What is the taste in your mouth? Do you taste grapes? Pineapples? Bones?

The AuralSec Story, A Corporate History, Chapter 7: Our Dependable Grampy

*The Seventh Chapter in the Story of the Rise of AuralSec, Inc.,
a Mobile Telecommunications Solutions Company, prepared in
preparation for the AuralSec Conclave, a gathering to celebrate
our company's achievements in our seventh year.*

We're celebrating victory after rolling out Version 2.0 of
the Dependable Grampy, a prepaid cellular telephone with a
single red button programmed to randomly call any one of ten
people on whom our imaginary customer, a very dependable
grampy, could call in case of an emergency, a twenty-first-
century I've-fallen-and-can't-get-up with the added twist that
our dependable grampy could also call any of his chosen ten
phone numbers at random just to chat, to talk about the Pirates
game or the weather or how the power people had come and
cut down the tree out front, assuming that our dependable
grampy would not care so much who he was calling, only that
he was calling somebody who would, on the other end of the
line, upon seeing his number, pick up the phone assuming the

worst: that our dependable grampy was calling because he had, in fact, fallen and could not get up, only to be surprised when he had only called to chat.

Version 1.0 of the Dependable Grampy was to be Aural Security Solutions' flagship product. The original Grampy included a self-defense feature and two buttons. The first button operated the emergency/lonely grampy feature as in version 2.0 and the second was the trigger for the stun gun feature originally marketed as a combined mobile telecommunications and self-defense solution for the dependable on-the-go elderly. While this product tested well, in the hands of actual customers it had less than stellar results as dependable grampies everywhere, trying to place a call, mistakenly hit the stun gun trigger either Tasing passersby, or, in several tragic cases (currently settled out of court) in which the dependable grampy pushed the button while holding the Dependable Grampy to his or her own ear, sending 50,000 volts through his thin grampy skull. Luckily for *those* dependable grampies, when and if they recovered, they were still holding their Dependable Grampy and were able to call for help. Our dependable grampy rarely made the mistake of hitting the stun gun trigger a second time and however much the product team pleaded with marketing and legal that dependable grampies would just have to learn how to use the damn phone, it was decided to pull the self-defense feature.

Jasper cuts the cake and passes plates around to general good cheer while we discuss our next product, a completely anonymous prepaid cellular telephone designed to compete with existing prepaid products sold in convenience stores and pawnshops: the Tweaker. The difference was that we would market these phones directly to drug dealers by employing a Tweaker street team who would hang around mall video game arcades and public parks pushing our products on drug dealers and their customers, extolling the virtues of a completely anonymous solution to their mobile telecommunications needs. We have high hopes for the Tweaker, and there's a lot of buzz floating around the company. The kind of buzz that incites us to pound our fists into each other's fists. We call this punching it in, and whenever somebody has a great idea or after a particularly satisfying lunch, we always punch it in.

The Tweaker has us all punching each other in. It's spring and winter had been long. Lawsuits were piling up. We needed a lift in morale, and the Tweaker has a lot of promise.

We are still working out how to demo the untraceability of the identity of the Tweaker's customers and whether or not to include a Dependable Grampy Version 1.0 stun gun feature when somebody knocks over a pitcher of water onto the fucking cake.

Jasper's phone buzzes on his belt and he leaves the office. It's his grandfather calling him from his Dependable Grampy 2.0. Jasper designed a lot of the features—it was his idea to make the stun gun button red. He claims that it's not his fault that people were hitting the red button when they wanted to hang up instead of when they wanted to defend themselves.

He suggested the default air-horn ringtone and personally picked the old man who played grampy in the television spots. So he should have suspected that his own grampy had fallen and couldn't get up, had swallowed his tongue, was mauled by dogs, etc. But Jasper knew better and sent him to voicemail. Grampy had Jasper's sister's kids with him for the weekend up at their little house in Pennsylvania. He'd either be calling to tell him that one of the kids had done something funny, that one of the kids had done something and he wasn't sure if what the kid had done would kill the kid, or to complain about how the strip miners came back after so many years and just tore the land behind his house a new asshole to scrape away what was left of the coal.

It's Phil that spilled the water on our fucking cake. We always do our cakes right and this cake was no exception. Three tiers with the airbrushed faces of our executives prematurely aged to fit the part, each talking on a Dependable Grampy. After Phil ruined the cake, the meeting's doomed. We don't talk any more about the Tweaker or the Phone Homeless (another prepaid product marketed toward the itinerant) but about how Phil is a fucking idiot, how somebody should bend Phil over, how maybe Jasper would punch Phil in the dick when Phil isn't expecting it because Denise had brought in the cake and even though we are all really disappointed the CEO isn't going to speak to us and let us feed him cake we shouldn't be pissed because he isn't going to show. Somebody suggests that we should all tear a new asshole in Phil. We were all really excited for cake. We're pretty sure there will be another one later in the day or tomorrow or the day after that, but still. We are so full of rage and self-loathing that punching each other helps us to validate that we are still humans, or close enough. Many of us have been forced to sign up for Gentle Hands Peacetime Violence Solution 2.0 seminars starting in two weeks to learn how to help make our hands gentle with one another.

We are also gearing up for the Conclave, our annual company retreat. This year, we are heading across the river to the Holiday Inn and looking forward to a day of trust falls and break-out sessions and our annual team trip to Medieval Times. The company always rents the whole place, and we mount up on horses and hit each other in the skulls with swords and jousting lances, and then our CEO passes out bags of frozen corn from a cooler for our heads and gives us a pep talk. Followed by a lot of illicit Conclave fucking in the darkest corners of the Holiday Inn.

Each one of us is personally held responsible for carrying out the CEO's wishes, and when we can't figure out how to do what he asks us to do, or when we do what he asks us to do and it is the wrong thing to do and it fails, we are punished. When we fail, we pick wooden chips out of a velvet punishment bag that sits in the empty human resources office and compare our chips to a chart to determine our punishment. Sometimes punishment is simple like not being able to wear jeans when we come in to work on Saturdays, but more often our punishment is having Minesweeper uninstalled from our computers or shaving our heads or no cake for a week. When we are asked to do something that is obviously impossible, like shipping a pallet of Dependable Grampy 3.0s to our warehouse in Pennsylvania when we haven't yet invented the 3.0, we call this putting square pegs in round holes. At first we relished the challenge of pushing square pegs into our superiors' round holes, but we tired quickly of visiting the punishment bag and so learned to argue about the impossibility of pushing square pegs into round holes. After a month of this tactic, management began to make us visit the punishment bag if we argued, so now we have learned to ask subordinates to push square pegs into round holes, who in turn pass the peg-pushing onto their subordinates and so on until the only people who have to visit the punishment bag are interns, because no matter how eager the interns are to please, it is very, very difficult to put square pegs into round holes.

The Wiz is what we call the CEO because he is a Wizard. He is sitting in a meeting now making up fake math on a whiteboard for two stunned junior executives from a major electronics retailer, trying to explain to them how they could relabel the remaining banned Dependable Grampy 1.0 units and package them with a belt clip and a holster, calling the result the Dependable Grampy Mini, assuring them that they can factory disable the stun gun feature (which is a lie) to make it functionally the same as the 2.0. He tells them not to be such pussies. As every salesman knows, this tactic will either work perfectly or backfire. In this case it works perfectly, and they agree to buy the remaining 1.0s, repackaged. The Wiz explains, too, that to save money on repackaging there are still at least twenty countries that have not banned the sale of the 1.0, so there are some options. Later, he will yell at the CIO and the warehouse manager until they reluctantly agree that what he has sold can be done, even though the three of them know it cannot. Then the CIO and the warehouse manager will have a meeting with their management teams and yell at them until they agree that it can be done even thought it can't. What will happen is that the major electronics retailer will receive the 1.0s in new boxes with the stun gun feature still enabled. Some grampy will buy the phone and electrocute his skull, and we will be sued, but we have very good lawyers. Perhaps the best. At least nobody will have to visit the punishment bag.

One of our junior lawyers, Denise, is no-nonsense about lawsuits. Our legal department is almost as big as our Office of the Chief Executive. We have more managers, directors, executive directors, senior directors, vice presidents, and chiefs per employee than any other company in the United States. We have almost as many lawyers. We have been sued or been charged with misrepresenting our products, false advertising, three kinds of Internet fraud, trafficking in controlled substances, manslaughter, sexual harassment, and tax fraud. All of these lawsuits are pending. Denise is in charge of making sure the lawsuits stay pending indefinitely.

When the Wiz goes to get coffee, he is going out to fuck his girlfriend, who is not his wife; he makes sure that everybody knows that he is going to get coffee. He walks the long way out of the building asking if anybody needs anything from Starbucks, and everybody knows that what he is really doing is going over to his girlfriend's place to fuck her. We call her Coffee. On days when he is going to get Coffee, he puts gel in his hair and leaves a little stubble. He has enormous feet and wears his pointy slip-on loafers and no socks. That's how amazing the Wiz is. He looks good. *Really* good.

When our CFO or CEO travel, they do so in a leased private jet. Those of us who remember the company in its earliest days remember the Wizard always dreamed of having a private jet for the company. The CFO likes to rent the jet and then a helicopter and then a private horse-drawn carriage to play golf with investors. He then tells them to go fuck themselves.

Some of us, when the Wizard is walking out to get Coffee and we see his stubble and those loafers, want to follow him to the elevator and pin him in there between floors and tear his shirt off and inhale his naked chest.

Last year at Conclave, in order to demonstrate the safety of the stun gun feature, the Wiz held a Grampy to the side of the CFO's head and Tased him. The CFO dropped to the ground and began to seize. While the Wiz illuminated the woeful media exaggerations as to the dangers of attack from an electroshock weapon, our CFO began to cry blood and foam black froth from his mouth. After the paramedics took the CFO away, the Wiz claimed that the injuries were a sign that we were on the right track. We decide that we will all hold a Grampy to our temples and hit stun as a sign of solidarity and loyalty and our belief in the will of the Wiz.

Every office has jargon that new employees must learn and adopt. Most people in the office have learned the phrases "don't be a pussy" and "I'm going to bend you over." Some employees used to complain to human resources about the use of these phrases. A memo was distributed and Sensitivity in the Workplace 2.0 training was arranged. So the Wiz got rid of human resources. The meaning of the phrases is this: "don't be a pussy" means "don't act like a cat" and "I'm going to bend you over" means "I'm going to force you into a prone position as if to fuck you in your anus." These are phrases that our sales guys call "power phrases."

Each year on the Wiz's birthday the Wiz tells his assistant what he would like for a gift, and then she raises the money from all the employees in the company. We are asked to donate what we can, but any of us that has any interaction with the Wiz knows that we must donate as much as possible to win his assistant's favor. Some of us have given as much as a week's pay and been rewarded by raises and promotions. We have raised enough money to buy the Wiz a very nice grill, a trip to Barbados, a fishing boat, and a hot air balloon. The employees take

shifts packing into the conference room for cake and to witness
the Wiz feigning surprise at the generous gift. He will hug us
and we will share cake. That is how much he loves us. We have
a similar competition to see who can buy the most Girl Scout
Cookies from the Wiz's kid during Girl Scout Season. We have
so many Girl Scout Cookie boxes stuffed away from previous
years that this year we went down and dumped them all in the
river to make room for new cookies.

Sometimes the Wiz helps another Denise (from marketing) try on dresses in the "executive men's room." It used to
be just the "executive restroom," but then the Wiz fired the
only female executive. He is working on finding a new one
because he knows how this looks, but in the mean time he likes
to call the little bathroom by his office the "executive men's
room" and likes to head in there an hour after lunch with the
sports section to look like he's taking a shit when he is actually
rubbing one out (on days when he is not going to get Coffee).
When we ask him what he was doing in the bathroom for so
long, he tells us that he was trying to figure out how to make
our numbers. So after Denise has been shopping in the afternoon, she comes back to the office with a bunch of new dresses,
and the Wiz offers to check them out so he follows her into the
executive men's room, and they're in there for about a minute
until she yells "go fuck yourself," and Wiz comes out and slinks
back to his office. Even though we know what the Wiz has
done is wrong, that much of what the Wiz does is wrong, we
know that we would have a tough time resisting the Wiz in

the executive men's room. We are both disgusted and ashamed at the Wiz's behavior, but we are all a little bit jealous that the Wiz does not follow us all into the executive men's room.

Some of us live by the mantra: "Well, at least nobody is going to die from what we do" even though that has allegedly happened at least five times. So when the Dependable Grampy 1.0 kills an elderly man in Pittsburgh, an elderly man who was not using his Dependable Grampy in an actual emergency situation, but a dependable grampy who was just calling to talk about the Pirates, we edit our mantra to be: "Well, at least nobody young is going to die from what we do." We feel especially bad about the elderly man because he died in the Squirrel Hill Tunnel around rush hour and caused many people to be very late. We talked about how we might customize a prepaid telephone offer for late commuters, an Emergency Commuting Telecommunications Solution, maybe something that they could depend on to signal to loved ones that they were late and on the way without actually initiating verbal communication with them. Unfortunately all of our phones already come with this feature, the "text message." Instead of a new product, we decide to launch an online advertising campaign and text-messaging onslaught to existing customers using the catchphrase: "Don't be such a pussy–call and let your partner know you're on the way."

We are all privately working on class action lawsuits against the company because some of us are afraid we will end up in jail. We would all like to be the first whistle blower. When we tell our Senior Executive Directors about our concerns, they acknowledge that yes, there is a good chance we will do some time if we keep doing what we are doing in terms of telling everybody to bend over and trying to make our numbers every month but that, oh man, what a ride it'll be. They ask us to consider the risks of suing our employer and point out the long backlog of lawsuits already in queue and suggest that even though jail time sounds like a real bummer, to weigh how much fun we will have over the next two years before all this shit hits the fan. And there is always the chance we will not get caught but get rich instead. They tell us that the last chapter has yet to be written on AuralSec and that no matter what, it will be big.

George in IT has been gearing up for Conclave for a while now, printing up the Conclave 2000 shirts. It is not 2000 anymore and hasn't been for years. The company wasn't even founded until 2002, but George likes the sound of Conclave 2000. We are all trying to convince our significant others to go to the Conclave dance, but they are mostly repulsed by our employers and coworkers. They remind us constantly that we could be making money elsewhere, and we have to remind them that it's going to be a great ride and that we can't really get off.

The way we make our numbers is this: there are websites on the internet devoted to gathering information in exchange for some small amusement. For example, enter your name and zipcode for a chance to win five hundred dollars. Enter your name and address to play a fun game where you throw monkeys off the roofs of buildings. We call these "sales leads," and at the end of the month we buy a bunch of leads from some odd folks up in New York who have mapped the raw data to enough customer data (addresses, social security numbers) that we can activate these "customers" on one of our wireless carrier partners and ship them a phone. We then make it impossible for these customers to return the phones. We will only accept their return within twenty-four hours of their initial interest in receiving a telephone, which is usually weeks or months ago.

Denise from finance has ordered blowguns in preparation for Conclave 2000. We do trust falls, of course, but the real trust, according to the Wiz, is for whom you are willing to take a bullet. Since we can't reasonably shoot each other with guns (we have had long, heated meetings to discuss how we might reasonably shoot each other with guns), we take darts for each other. We line up in rows with our backs to our colleagues, and they fire darts into our necks, backs, and buttocks from the blowguns. The darts hurt like hell but that is how we learn to really trust each other. We hold Dependable Grampies to our skulls and hit the stun gun button just to show how fucking devoted we are to AuralSec. We will do it again this year and like every year, we will awaken to sheet cakes.

The Wiz caught the CFO fucking the Wiz's assistant, also named Denise, in the CFO's office once. This was an awkward moment because the Wiz had been trying to fuck Denise for years, but she was never interested. We do not understand how she resists the Wiz, so we believe that she is playing hard to get. So when the Wiz caught her with the CFO after lunch one afternoon, he wasn't so much angry as oddly hurt as she is his right-hand woman. She is his confidant. His eyes and ears. They used to go to concerts together and sway in the darkness whispering the lyrics to each other. She may run the company. Part of him loves her and seeing her there on the CFO's desk, black pantyhose around her thighs, the tube socks and commuter sneakers, something emptied a little inside him, like she was no longer his, even though she had never been.

We all love the Wiz's wife, also named Denise, even though we wish we were Coffee. Sometimes the Wiz's wife comes in with the kids, and she is smart and gorgeous, and we wonder why she is married to the Wiz. She has some sort of engineering degree the Wiz likes to say. One of their kids, the smallest one, comes to the office one day with the Wiz's wife. His name is Ichabod. There is a silence because it sounds like it could be a joke but nobody will laugh because there is a real chance that the Wiz has named his son Ichabod. We nod waiting for the joke, and when we think it is safe, we tell him it is an awesome fucking name and that we all wish we had thought of it first. Several of us silently plan to also name our soon-to-be-born children Ichabod. Denise smiles the kind of smile that suggests to us that no matter how much she thinks Ichabod is an okay name, the Wiz convinced her that Ichabod was the best name in the world and the fact that this kid will grow up to be Ichabod Wizard scares the shit out of her. Two weeks later somebody asks Wiz, "Hey, how's Ichabod," and the Wiz says "Who?" and the person says "Ichabod, your smallest child, the soft one," and the Wiz says, "I'm sorry, I don't know who you're talking about. My son's name is Noah."

We sometimes get close to admitting to ourselves that the Wiz is probably a felon, and that when things go down, many of us will go down with him. Some of us find new jobs, but when we find new jobs and tell the Wiz, the Wiz tells us that we are dead to him, and even though we might be better off being dead to the Wiz, the thought of it frightens us. We do not want to find out what it is like to not have him in our lives. Today we are working on a new product, the Bodywatch, a mobile death alert solution designed for elderly women who live alone to prevent their pets from eating them should they die in their apartments. Bodywatch customers will be called at intervals of their choosing and be greeted with a prerecorded message to which the customer must respond in the positive: "Yes, I am still alive." When a customer doesn't respond, we will send the paramedics and somebody to take care of the cats until arrangements can be made. When the Wiz shows up at the end of our meeting to see what we've come up with, we'll whiteboard it out for him and feed him cake.

Animal Attacks

A single brown nail bent works its way from a single length of brittle timber. A row of crows watch as the timber falls. Hear that scraping above their heads, a falcon tearing at power lines. Sparks fizzle falling and burn our hair. Hear those chickens clucking away shaking their crates about to fall from the back of the truck and scatter across the highway lanes.

Hear an ice cube drop into another drink. A ladder dropped against aluminum siding for us to climb and clear away the gutter junk and possums and squirrels. Hear them turning over the trashcans at night.

Hear the twitch of the lighter.

All the birds conspiring against us jamming jet engines and taking down choppers.

The raccoon the size of a dog is not just watching.

The cat clawing at my chest trying to steal my breath at night. The cat's lips pressed against mine her eyes staring into mine. Later the cat warm next to the long iguana stretched across the top of the couch looking at me when I come home from work and the two of them have been alone together all day.

The dog pulling at his leash trying to take us into traffic. The fish biting my hands when I clean their tank. The fish jumping out of the tank onto the tangle of power cords trying to sizzle the strip and burn down the house when we are alone for the weekend.

The spiders crawling up from the basement on hot nights crawling into our mouths and burrowing deep in our throats.

When you fell off the side of the raft white watering down the Zambezi I could see in your eyes that you thought I wanted to leave you there in the brown water for the crocodiles and bull sharks and brown water full of parasites.

Glossary

AA: Ascending the Allegheny Mountains. Sitting by a window in Noah's Ark, formerly the S.S. Grand View Point Hotel, looking out over the valley, able to spot seven counties and three states.

AA: Alcoholics Anonymous is founded on June 10, 1935.

AA: Cracked glass and vines and twenty pink leather cocktail chairs on their sides. A blue vase, a curtain. A shredded curtain.

AA: On July 1, 1979, he forces himself head first down an eight-inch wide hole in the backyard of his aging mother and father. Like a worm he pushes first his head and then his body into the earth and slithers into darkness.

AA: Here he enjoys his last drink on June 10, 1978.

AA: Competes on television game shows and eats adult foods to the astonishment of audiences.

AA: Ends career by demonstrating a one-handed bra unhooking on a morning talk show.

AA: On July 1, 1981.

AA: Ascending the Allegheny Mountains at night. No radio stations, only the sound of no one speaking. Only broken light from headlights passing and the dashboard. Make this night forever.

AAA: The American Association of Aphorisms is founded on July 10, 1950. Lost time is never found again. A lie told often enough becomes the truth.

AAA: The American Association of Advertising Agencies is founded on July 10, 1917.

AAA: The American Automobile Association is founded on June 4, 1902, in Cleveland, OH, and is responsible for the invention of.

AAA: Headlights around a traffic circle. A faint and distant ring system. A circle of cigarettes smoked. An empty cup coffee-stained brown.

AAA: A misplaced folder of photographs.

AAA: The Agricultural Adjustment Act of June 12, 1933, restricted farmers by reducing them, cropping them to raise their surplus value, thereby relative farmers.

AAAA: Smaller than AAA.

AAAA: He did ask her to dance and she did say no. It is more complicated. He sees her first at an all-ages punk show at the Ebensburg, Pennsylvania, Fire Hall. She is wearing a tight black dress and smiles at him, lifting the edge of her hem to reveal the top of her thigh-high black and white striped tights. Her hair is bleached and straight. She looks like a hot witch.

AAAAA: Ascend the mountain.

Aircraft Carriers: A unique aircraft carrier.

Airships: Rigid airships.

Akron, OH: On June 12, 1978, the "City of Angels" burned to the reduction of artificial application of water to the soil.

Akron, OH: Forty miles east of Akron, OH, in a forest on a hill.

Akureyri: Show me cold water flowing and

Alan Alda: Badly burned on June 1, 1980, while freebasing cocaine.

Alan Alda: A sinkhole opens in a valley to one black cavern glistening. Cold black water glistens.

Altoona, PA: The demand for locomotives during the Civil War stimulated much of this growth, and by the later years of the war, a valuable city. Downtown Altoona is notable for having several churches. Crumble into dust. See also Robitussin.

Ann Arbor Railroad: Founded on June 1, 1997, the Ann Arbor Railroad is the largest in the United States and connects the towns.

Amusements: An empty box falls from the top of a dresser. Frays of paper like streamers fall from the box onto the floor. Below the floor a single bent nail falls from a floor joist onto the basement floor.

Archaeopteryx: The First Bird.

Athletics: Despite being a goth she is an excellent synchronized swimmer.

BB: He asks her to dance but she keeps singing, the tips of her fingers on the edge of her hem.

BB: The world's first uniformed youth organization.

BB: Combines drills and fun activities with values. Habits of obedience, reverence, discipline, self-respect towards projectiles. After the birdshot pellet of approximately the same size.

BB: Four teacups full of dirt stacked in a row on a wooden shelf, a bare brick wall behind them.

BB: Strategic trackage in Central Virginia.

B and B: Equal parts Benedictine and cognac. Founded on June 25, 1924, with offices in Liberty, Salisbury, and Fulton.

BBB: A defect heart's membranic conduction system structure which acts primarily to protect the blood brain from brain chemicals in the blood, a defect of the heart's electrical conduction system.

BBB: Founded on June 25, 1912. Not a government but an effective network undertaking long distance migrations. Many more perform shorter irregular movements. Communicates using signals, including cooperative breeding and mobbing of predators. Usually, disputes can be resolved through mediation; the vast majority are socially monogamous, usually for one breeding season, sometimes for years.

BBB: Rarely for life.

BBB: Columns, a car, a broom.

BBB: Others have breeding systems that are polygynous ("many females") or, rarely, polyandrous ("many males"). Complaints about the practice of professions like medicine, law and accounting are usually not handled by eggs laid in a nest and often incubated. The organization's dispute resolution procedures are established by a council of locals, and implemented by locals. When appropriate, low or no-cost arbitration may also be offered and provided by regulating associations.

Barberry: A flowering shrub.

Bee: A fundamental light system is a modern aircraft in that it controls the navigation.

Bird: Somewhere.

Bird: Cage wires and falls through trees, falling, shattering.

Bramble: On their backs in the warm sand looking at the night sky he touches her hand.

Brine: Analyses using high-spatial-resolution hyperspectral imaging. Damaged concrete.

Bulldozer: Breaking curfew they drive deep into the sinking valley, the ground rolling like soft waves of water. Gentle motion.

Business: Popular railroading marvel. In 1986, high on Robitussin, three teenagers manage to derail a train by removing a section of track with crowbars.

CC: A pool of light gathers in the gray space.

CC: Everything has turned to dust.

CCC: Prepaid cellphone, a box of lawnmower parts, a bag of live crickets, cricket habitat.

CCC: Resembles the source of a large, steep sided far side. Is an opening.

Cambria: Fantasy Forest, Storybook Forest, Fairytale Forest, Forest Zoo, The Fairytale Tavern, Fantasy Mountain Cocktail Lounge, The Forest Lounge. The Old Woman's Shoe Cocktail Lounge and Inn. Gas station shaped like tea kettle. Gas station shaped like elephant. Wooden teeth museum. Elephant collectable museum. Taxidermy museum. Hotel shaped like ark. Bar shaped like old woman's shoe. Hotel built inside railroad caboose. Convenience stores.

Cambridge, MA: A private institution of higher learning in Cambridge, MA. Also: Ex-Junkie (one dog). Fifteen active junkies crowded into a bungalow (dog lovers, but no dog). Six junkies, three dogs, nightly bonfires.

Cleveland, OH: Cleveland, OH was the site of the first nuclear detonation on July 16, 1945.

Crack Lung: Symptoms include numbness and burning and waking at night. Can be managed effectively with nighttime wrist splinting. The index finger, the middle finger, the ring finger, the thumb, the little finger. Sometimes the palm. Sometimes other fingers as well.

Crickets: Somewhat have bodies. Insects somewhat related to grasshoppers and more closely related to katydids or. Somewhat have flattened bodies. Crickets in a cricket habitat chirp pleasant cricketing all night and bring the deepest sleep.

Crickets: Invention of beer. Invention of zipper. First known baseball. First steam ferry. Demonstration of steam locomotive. First electrified commuter train. Invention (acci-

dental) of soft ice cream. First automated parking garage.
First sandwich restaurant. First public central air conditioning. First wireless phone system. Invention of toast.
Invention of oranges. Invention of the color orange. Home
of the waffle cone. Here on a hill he asks her to marry
him. A cricket pleasant on his leg. The hazy sky. Neither
of them actually tremble. Sunbathers bathe on every green
inch. So many they could walk across the river, sailboat to
sailboat. The elderly and infirm drop dead.

CWRY: Main office in Wilroy.

D: Founded in June.

D: The trunk of an abandoned Buick full of bungee cords
and jumper cables and ten feet of thick chain and two old
tires shredded into thin strips of rubber ignites.

D: We sit in the car in darkness and wait.

DD: Founded in 1951.

The Board Game Monopoly

When I get home I try to unlock the door before anybody notices me. Shelly's on her stoop with her face in her hands. I want to slide by.

She tells me her 12-year-old kid Brian came home and started yelling at her that she had demons in her and told her he was going to cut her throat. He wanted to get rid of the demons, but he can't get rid of them.

That's why they're demons.

Her quiet friend, the one that never says anything, puts down her beer and says, "We were just playing Monopoly. The board game Monopoly?"

I nod. I've heard of it.

"Shelly was too drunk to go get him at the skateboard park—she was being responsible."

This makes sense to me.

"He had to walk home and came in swinging. We were just playing Monopoly. The board game Monopoly? Then he told her he was going to cut her throat. It's a good thing she took his knife away from him."

That's what it's like here. Monopoly. The board game Monopoly.

She tells me again that Shelly was just being responsible. It's not right to drink and drive. She'd had three 24 oz. Natural Ices. She was doing the right thing by asking him to walk. It's 95 degrees and the skateboard park's only five miles, but she was drunk and they were playing the board game Monopoly, and it wasn't late. It was almost six o'clock. I go inside.

On Saturday morning Shelly tells me she's going to make amends. She's going to landscape the yard. She's tired of the dirt, tired of the dog lying in the dirt. It makes the dog sad, it makes her kid sad, it makes her sad. It makes her house filthy. She's tired of black spots on the clean white carpet.

So she's going to landscape the yard, put in stepping-stones, build up a little hill against the house and plant flowers, maybe some of that ornamental grass. Brian's going to come over and she's not going to tell him because it's going to be a surprise. He hates her house, hates the yard, hates the dirt. His demons hate the dirt and the dog drooling all over the place. She told me to stay away from the dog's drool because it's toxic. It melted the paint off of her Buick.

She tells me she's going to take charge. She's in control, she's always been in control. She's going to make it nice for her, her dog, and her son and she's going to see more of her son, maybe keep him at her place so she can make sure he's taking his medication. The medication pushes his demons deep down inside.

Later I hear them going at it again. I stand on the porch and listen. The guy across the street is raking his leaves onto the front porch of the vacant house next door. He told me he doesn't want new neighbors. I wonder if Brian's really attacking his mom.

I hear her telling Brian she's going to send him home in a cab, which I can't believe, but there it is in front honking the horn. She pushes her flailing kid into the backseat, stroking his head, telling him it's for his own good.

After she's given the cab driver money and he drives her son away, she looks at her dog, a big slow bloodhound with two strands of drool hanging out of his mouth.

"I think I'm going to have the dog put down."

After she goes inside, three raccoons approach the house. They emerge from different vantage points across the street— from below a car, from beneath a porch, from the sewer drain. They have a strategy for whatever it is that they want. The raccoons are the size of dogs and when I stand to scare them their leader sits up on its hind legs and hisses at me, thrashing its claws. I back away from them and go inside. From my living room window I can no longer see them.

I lie in bed and hear the raccoons on the roof scratching at the shingles.

Shelly told me when I moved in she saw the lesbians three houses down shooting up on their porch one night around dinner time when she was coming back from the corner store with beers. She told her son they were diabetic, just sitting on the porch injecting insulin together on a nice fall day. That's what lesbian diabetics do.

Usually when I drive home late at night the lesbians are either sitting around a little bonfire they've built in their front yard drinking beer while one of them stands in the middle of the road juggling torches or spinning a long pole with flaming ends. When I get to their house I slow down and wait for the person with the flames to move out of the street and wave at them.

Nothing too serious, but if you are playing with fire in the street you are advertising to the world that you are high on drugs. They don't bother me. They are young and when I was young, I too wasted evenings wasted on the porch playing with fire.

I come home to the cops and my neighbor chain smoking on her stoop next to a paper bag heavy with beer. The last time this many police visited the block was when the old man on the corner broke his hip. He'd fallen on his space heater, which burned him in half.

This time it's the refugees across the street. Something about the mother's boyfriend coming and beating up the kids, punching the mother. That sort of thing. My neighbor's had enough, so she called the cops.

The police gather around their cars in their shorts and whisper. The woman across the street stands next to her back door sobbing into her hands. Two men argue on the corner. A voice crackles from the Taco Time drive through across from the pawnshop. A baby cries out.

Shelly's afraid for her life. She tells me about something years ago, her mother holding some kid captive in the basement for weeks, then the police taking the kid away in handcuffs. I get these things in pieces. She laughs into her beer. So somebody's after her. They unscrewed three of her lug nuts. I start to say that if they really wanted to kill her they would probably remove all of her lug nuts, but she's telling me now this guy across the street always hassling the refugees is bad news and she's heard things about him from the mother and she's got to watch her back. She knows when people are messing with her.

When I come home a man dressed as a shepherd carrying a shepherd's staff with the curly-q tip throws a Wendy's bag into my yard and flips me off. I think it's the same shepherd who yesterday wanted me to cosign a loan for him at the pawnshop around the corner to buy the dirt bike he was test-driving. I tried to explain to him that I had things to do, how there was no time for me to help him, but he shook his staff at me and said I had nothing to do and he needed my help. He was right. There is nothing for me to do.

At midnight, I come home from driving around looking at the city lights from up on the hill to see two of the lesbians stumbling up the sidewalk. I find my keys and hurry to the front door.

"Hey, we want to welcome you to the neighborhood."

I'd moved in over a year ago.

One of them is carrying a bottle of wine wrapped in what looks like a velvet wizard's bag. They hand it to me and I undo the drawstring and nod approvingly at the wine they've chosen. The bottle is dusty and the white label is stained brown.

I notice the wine is already open and missing a glass or two. I unscrew the lid and take a drink from the bottle. The wine is thick and bitter. I offer them the bottle and they shake their heads.

"We've had plenty."

We sit in silence on the porch for a few minutes. I keep drinking from the bottle waiting for them to say something. I start to say that I'm tired and have things to do even though I don't have anything to do when one says, "Do you like to party?"

I know what it means when people ask me if I like to party. I tell them I don't.

"Can you score us some coke tonight?"

I have no idea how to score them some coke tonight, but I like to be helpful so before telling them no I look up at the porch ceiling like I'm rolling through my mental Rolodex considering who might be home tonight and have some spare cocaine that I could score for my neighbors.

I tell them sorry, I just can't think of anybody who can score some cocaine and start to explain that I'm sort of new in the area and that if we were in my hometown I could totally score them whatever they wanted just like that. I thank them for the wine and tell them I'll keep an eye out for some blow. I feel like I should give the wine back to them because they look disappointed as they say goodbye with their heads low to go back to the other lesbians gathered on their lawn.

Shelly tells me she loves the girl across the street, the little refugee who steals cigarette butts out of my ash tray enough nights I've started to leave her a few unsmoked Camels so she doesn't have to smoke burned butts. In the morning they're gone. I see her sneaking out of her basement window running barefoot across the street where she's hidden her cigarette stash under a white Toyota that hasn't moved in weeks. We nod to one another like old drinking pals.

The little girl had started to come over to play with the dog and Shelly had invited her inside to watch television, then started to make dinner for her and her little brothers. On Friday nights her son Brian comes over and the little girl across the street comes over and they watch movies late eating popcorn and falling asleep on the couch.

After a few weeks of this, Shelly wants to adopt the little girl. She offered the kid's mother five grand, but the mother refused because she can't give up the girl because she takes care of the little boys, too, so there's no deal unless she takes the girl and one of her infant brothers. Shelly's broken up over this, because she can handle a ten-year-old, but not a ten-year-old and a toddler. I tell her she's lucky she can afford two children and she should count her blessings.

I sit on the porch at dusk and watch a woman blow a man in his car, then give him a hug goodbye before getting out to get in her own car. She waves at me and smiles and I raise a can of beer to her. Later I sit on my old couch and watch television through a cloud of little black flies spinning in circles between me and *Project Runway*. When I go outside to sit on the porch, my neighbor is there at the fence about to call my name to talk. I sit down and settle in for the night.

When I don't see Shelly on Sunday morning or after lunch or into the evening and her hound's been in the entryway to her house looking dead all day, the door cocked open and flies floating over his body, I think Shelly's poisoned herself and the dog in some sort of weird suicide pact. I think I should head over there and see if she's okay but part of me is happy because I think if she's dead she probably won't talk to me as much.

She emerges at dusk and swings the garden hose around spraying water onto the dirt where she will one day have her grass and a little hill with flowers.

A couple nights a week I sit on my couch in the dark and listen to cats fighting in my backyard, grateful for some sound coming out of the silent night. One night one of the cats starts to say "oh boy oh boy oh boy oh boy" and I realize what I'm listening to is not cats fighting but the neighbor on the other side of my house having sex with his girlfriend. I sit on my couch in the dark and listen to them getting it on. After they finish I sit on the porch and watch him lead her out to his car, resting his lips on her cheek to say goodbye.

Shelly puts in grass and builds a little mound out of stones in the middle of the tiny yard. The mound looks like one of those roadside monuments people build to mark the place where a loved one died on the highway. Three sad flowers bend out of the stones.

"Does this look like a grave to you?"

"No, it looks like a feature to me. A magnificent feature."

"I think it's cute."

She ran out of sod halfway through so instead of getting more she left an odd L-shaped patch of dirt next to her sidewalk.

"Look how happy he is. He loves his new yard." She nods toward her dog standing on the patch of grass next to the grave. She turns on the hose again spraying down the grass and the dog. He jumps a little under his giant weight, wags his tail, and raises his nose into the stream of cool water.

Shelly tells me the lesbians have arrest records for burglary. I have no idea how she knows this, but I bristle, because I have been burgled at previous addresses and don't want to be burgled again. Shelly says the neighborhood is going to hell. Brian found a paper bag full of guns hidden in the fork of a tree behind the elementary school. She told him to put the guns back in the tree.

I see one of the lesbians feeding the dog through the fence and am suspicious they are trying to befriend him so when they do break in he will think they are his friends and leave them alone. I decide to keep an eye on those lesbians.

I come home around nine on a Friday from the Wal-Mart and there are so many cops on the street I can't get through, so I have to drive around the block and park in front of the pawnshop and the leather place. I'm a little annoyed because I have all this shit in these Wal-Mart bags and have to carry them a few houses down to my house, unhook the bungee cords that hold the fence together, and carry this shit up the stairs. I ask Shelly what's going on, even though I know what's going on because I see the car the cops are about to impound belongs to the hooker that I like to wave to when she's around. She looks at me through the window of the police car and smiles just like always. I give her a little wink.

"I got sick of all the hooking," she says.

The cops have the hooker's stuff spread out on the hood of their car. They pick at the make-up and syringes like kids hovering over Halloween candy. One of the cops empties a crumpled brown bag and holds up the gun that slides out like it's a stuffed parrot he's won at the claw machine.

"I came home and she was blowing this guy again."

I don't mention that sometimes I watch her blowing the guys. When there's something to watch, I'm grateful for it.

She tells me how her sister was murdered when she was twenty-one and into drugs and hooking and how she can't let it happen again and makes another reference to the guy her mother kept locked up in the basement for all those years, how the media didn't give her a break so why should she give anybody a break especially with how her sister died and her deadbeat brother sold her out and how she's broken her mother's steam cleaner and her mother's going to be pissed even though her mother owes her for all the times she's paid off her Penney's card. I wait. She tells me when the cops came they were just going to write the two of them up for lewd behavior but noticed a sandwich bag full of pills on the dashboard they just couldn't ignore no matter how much they would rather be filling up 40 oz coffee thermoses at the 7-Eleven. So they searched her and found more pills, syringes, the handgun. So the cops have been doing whatever it is cops have to do in a situation like this: talking it through with the other cops, searching, prodding, standing around the scene soaking it all in, taking notes. One of the cops starts taking photographs of the road around the car. Two more cops show up on their bicycles and watch in their shorts and helmets.

From my bedroom window I can see the little girl from across the street open one of Shelly's basement windows and crawl inside.

From the porch I watch her toss one of Shelly's 24 oz Natural Ice beers out of the window and shimmy out. With the beer in hand she skips between our houses and hops the fence, running across the street to climb down into her own basement window. A few minutes later she comes out to grab a smoke from beneath the white Toyota.

Shelly's been in another accident. Somebody ran her off the road and her tire came off and she doesn't know where the money's going to come from. Her boyfriend Craig broke up with her after he drove down to Vegas with his friends and fucked a waitress. That's why he had to break up with her, because of the waitress, but Shelly thinks his friends have talked him out of dating an older woman. She loves him. The little girl across the street has been breaking into her house and her car stealing candy and eating her food and trashing her house. She found one of her kitchen stools down in the basement so the little girl could climb out of the window she'd unlocked.

I start to say oh yeah I totally saw her breaking into your house and she steals my cigarette butts but I don't.

Shelly tried to talk to the little girl's mother, but nobody will answer the door over there, so the little girl isn't allowed to come to her house anymore. She never knocked, Shelly says. She should know better. Craig's going to come over even though they've broken up and install new locks and put bars on the basement windows. Shelly's worried anyway, because of her car accident, the lug nuts, the candy wrappers littering her basement floor. Somebody's after her. The people across the street, she says, know some bad people who do bad things. And the hooker. She's afraid she's gone too far.

When there is no sound, when there is only the sound of something humming from within the house, something scratching on the roof trying to get in, something scurrying through hidden spaces, I sit on the cold kitchen floor in darkness and wait for silence. Shrill oh boy oh boy oh boys prick through the closed windows. I put my hands over my ears and listen to what I imagine is thick black blood oozing through my veins. I imagine guns hidden in a tree, imagine all of the aspirin in the jumbo Wal-Mart tub in the cupboard lined up like ants snaking across the floor, imagine my house aflame. My thumbs fall asleep. A light goes on next door and shines across the kitchen floor.

We sit on the porch and drink tall cans of Natural Ice. Autumn is beginning and we listen to the chestnuts falling from the trees, hitting our cars like baseballs falling from heaven. Flames from a forest fire consume a town in the next county and the wind has carried the smell of burning houses to our neighborhood.

Shelly's afraid. She says she should move into her old house, move back with her ex-husband who lied and cheated on her and now spends all day at the gym or the tanning salon. She tells me it would make her life easier to dump her boyfriend who is never around and twenty years younger and suck it up and forgive her ex-husband for cheating and move into her house up in the foothills. That house has fourteen foot cathedral ceilings and lapis lazuli tile in the bathroom that she did herself and sits on a third of an acre with a wooden fence and has plenty of room for her dog to run around and be happy. She would be happy. Her son would be happy. Everybody wants them to get back together, but she's in love with this younger guy who works with her at the Home Depot and tells her he loves her and wants to have children with her and move in and make things right.

"Lapis lazuli is the expensive shit," she says.

I nod.

"The problem with Craig." She takes a drink from his beer.

"You'd like him. He has tats and great hair. I'm sure you've seen his ridiculous truck parked in front of the house."

I've never seen his truck and still contend that Craig is imaginary.

"You're a good listener."

She goes in to get "her smokes" and returns with two Natural Ices and tosses one over the fence to me. It hits the concrete porch and the beer gurgles inside the can. I pick it up and tap the top and laugh while she starts to tell me about the time she saw Pink Floyd.

"I've seen all the greats. Journey, Styx, the Doobies. I met Ray Stevens at Cracker Barrel and he signed my jeans jacket, and I got King Diamond to sign my jeans across the ass when I met him on the train. He really liked that. My ass was a lot smaller then. That was before he was really famous. I've got the jeans and the jeans jacket framed together and up in the dining room. I sliced my hand open on a kitchen knife once and met Kenny Loggins at the emergency room, but he wouldn't give me an autograph. He's a dick."

I look for raccoon eyes hidden in the shadows.

"I'll have to show you my autograph collection. I'll have you over for dinner and we can look through my photo albums. I have a lot of signatures. Ray Stevens, King Diamond, most of Styx. Everyone."

A guy stumbles up to the neighbor's trashcan across the street and drops in a can.

"Get the fuck away from there."

The guy looks over and says, "I was just tossing my can."

"Well, you tossed it, now get the fuck going. I don't want to see you around here."

The guy is skeletal.

"I'll let my fucking dog tear the shit out of you, you skinny shit. Move the fuck on."

Shelly's dog barks a long, low woof from inside. The guy shakes his head and keeps walking.

"They're giving me a hard time at work, did I tell you the latest? My boss told me I need to start covering up my tits better because the girls who work up front are jealous. Can you believe it?"

I wonder if the raccoons might try to climb down the chimney.

"They're the ones that are all doing their nails all day and talking about their hair and I'm just doing my job and then he starts talking about my tits. They're all jealous because of Craig. He's younger than all of them and he loves me. He's all tatted up and has long blond hair. They all want him. He doesn't care if I'm twenty years older. He told me he'd even go in with me if I wanted to adopt that little girl. So they want me to start covering my tits better and I told that son-of-a-bitch I wanted a raise and that it's hot in the back and all I do is sit in that shithole by myself all day and I don't give a rat's ass what the fuck the girls in the front care about my tits."

I hear the guy on the other side of the house with his girlfriend. "Oh boy oh boy oh boy oh boy oh boy."

"That fucker gave me another two fifteen an hour and told me I could wear whatever I god-damned want. He's lucky I don't sue his ass for looking at my tits all day. You know what you should do?"

During the pause I listen to the quiet: crickets, the sound of somebody ordering drive through at Taco Time, traffic. Soft oh boys rippling through the air. I pray for a gun shot in the distance to distract the conversation.

"You should write a book on how to talk to women. You're an expert."

If only this were true.

"Seriously, I'm not blowing smoke up your ass. That book would really be something."

"I just like to listen."

"I wish Craig were more like you. I wish I had a boyfriend like you."

She laughs it off and says she doesn't really want a boyfriend like me, that Craig's great but doesn't like to eat anything but plain hamburgers with ketchup. When they go to the Sizzler all he wants is a plain hamburger with ketchup and a baked potato with butter and sour cream and a Coke. He won't even drink a beer.

"I've got arm cancer," she says.

I'm not sure I believe in arm cancer.

"I've had it for years, but the doctors say it's spreading." She motions up and down her arm. "I don't feel anything, though. I don't trust doctors. They want me go see a specialist, but I'm going to let it ride. If it were cancer, I'd feel something."

I say goodbye while she's still talking.

Inside, I sit in my little front room. Something buzzes around my head.

"Are you dead in there?" she says through the screen door.

Shelly comes inside and says she wants to show me something. She sits next to me on the couch and hands me a rock. The rock is gray and green with threads of gold. She and Brian had gone rock hunting up in one of the valleys and he'd found it in the sand, right there on the surface.

"That's not fool's gold." She takes a deep breath. "It's real."

She says Brian's going to come home with a whole bucket full. I tell her it's beautiful.

We sit listening to the chestnuts fall outside, breathing the faint smoke from distant burning homes.

In the morning I hit the snooze bar eleven times before I decide to face the day. I hear what sounds like a truck horn and a dog barking and walk out onto the porch wrapped in my robe and look for the truck. On the sidewalk, facing up the street, a couple sits on two folded chairs. The man has a big white beard and his long hair curls from beneath his pioneer hat. They've got tan suede vests and she's got bright light blue pajama bottoms on and those garden clogs with the holes in them that everybody is wearing. They sit staring up the street without speaking, the man occasionally blowing into a little horn like a bugle that sounds like a truck's horn. Without speaking she takes a drink from a Diet Coke bottle, rises and folds her chair and waits for him to do the same, then follows him single file up the middle of the street in lockstep. I admire how early in the morning they've gotten up to do this thing and imagine them spending the whole day at it, sitting, blowing their horn, and marching on.

The Sodding

When we hadn't seen the dog for three days I asked Father where had the dog gone. He looked into his empty glass, looked at me, and handed me the glass. I knew what to do. When I returned I asked him again what had happened to the dog. He took a long drink from his glass and asked "What dog?"

In the backyard we dig a pit where we hadn't already dug a pit and my brothers pile into it. With the shovel I throw dirt onto them and when they are covered they push their arms menacingly out of the dirt. Next their heads and shoulders. They moan like zombies. Next pit it will be my turn to be a zombie.

When mother goes out for a bag of potatoes for mashed potatoes and doesn't come back for three days my brothers begin to weep because they miss Mother. Father is throwing a bag of ice against the concrete driveway. I ask him where Mother went and when were we going to have mashed potatoes and he tells me that he doesn't know how to make that. When I ask him if he suspects foul play he tells me that my brothers and I have ruined the yard.

Father pulls up in his big truck and the back is full of grass rolled into rolls stacked neatly in rows. We form a chain of grass haulers and pass bundles of grass one to the other to the backyard and Father rakes the soil level and begins to spread the grass. When it's late we sit on the back porch with cold lemonades and admire our handiwork even though there is much work to be done.

When Father tells us that he's going out for groceries we know what this means and give him big teary hugs. He acts like he doesn't know why we're so sad, all us kids on him. He'll be right back.

Pastoral

that roots the blast explodes the leaves, the tree is my destroyer

A rumbling and snow drifts from gray trees. Winter geese gray and shuddering in their sleep crane their gray tree necks. Feathers fall from trees. Fall into the snow piled on the ground. The snow piled on the ground shakes and settles, shaken. Thick light approaches the frozen field and bounces the carnival blue. The Swinger swings hang silent and blue. The Century Wheel gondolas swing slowly in the slow light, blue.

She's is wearing a black dress.
The television for a moment
blue.

Hot soot bubbles through the snow, blooming dirt through the frozen crust. A maintenance man in a blue uniform taps a shovel against the crust shaking the soil rods into crumbles. The rumble rumbles and everything crumbles into dust. He looks up.

A raptor huddles in its cage hoisted high above and eats its own long frozen eggs cracking each shell with beak tip, sucking the thick, cold yoke. One it swallows whole and one rolls from the nest and falls through the cage wires and falls through trees and wires, falling, shattering on the hard ground.

She's wearing a black dress and Cartier sunglasses cover her eyes. She's fallen across the hotel bed in the room the only light distant disasters in the silent television. He pushes his fingers into her hair a beautiful

mess.
rumble and a slow, wet snow
dragging down the gray, trees, geese winter and
shuddering in sleep
geese craning their necks
feathers fall from the tree. Falls of snow piled on the ground.

The snow is piled earth and descends, shake, shake, shake. Thick frozen light and a field of Carnival returns to blue. The mercurial hanging on quietly and blue. Century wheel gondolas swing

slow light, green.

Her Cartier sunglasses over her eyes, her arms crossed behind her head. The glow from the television the residue of devastation on her face. A black dress. He stands naked at the foot of the bed.

The Century Wheel, mercurial hanging, shakes loose bolts, gondolas swinging. Screws unwind. There is no wind. The ground vibrates. A star appears in the sky behind thick clouds. Three blue plates painted pastoral fall from a wall and shatter. A milk glass falls off the edge of a table and shatters. A woman on her way to work falls down stairs and breaks her ankle. A woman on her way to work pushing an earring through a hole in her earlobe falls down stairs and breaks her ankle. Tears her earlobe. A deer walking across a frozen pond falls through the thin ice cracking and drowns. A man walking across his living room falls across a space heater.

His watch falls. He watches the screen flickering scenes and remembers the first time they huddled against one another in the black theater burrowing their hands into each other's hands trying to push through skin to get inside watching the first of many movies. He remembers what it was like to know what was real. The bright bodies bent around one another above them. Fingers. The skin beneath the edge of her sweater.

Her Cartier sunglasses over her eyes, her arms crossed behind her head. He stands at the foot of the bed and tries to remember the color of her eyes. She motions for him to move as the ground swallows a man on the screen.

through the green fuse drives the green age, that the root causes of a tree is my devastator

Carnival rides collapse: It's a Small World, The Adult Teacup, The Broken Home, The Century Wheel, The Colossus,
The Crazy Bus, The End of Days,

The end of fun.

          mercurial   , shakes   swing-
ing.   unwind.   no wind.   vibrates.
cloud. Three blue plates painted pastoral   .
and shatters. A woman   .
A woman

                      breaks

.

                      unhumps

. Humping. A deer
    drowns. A man
            burns in half.

The Century Wheel rolls from its mooring, rolls across the
snow, rolls

The water-rock
Passing the flow of red
   wax.

They know each other better than anyone can claim to
know another person and yet. He is helpless. He stands at the
foot of the bed. Fragments in the glass fade in and then away.
Moments and another moment and nothing.

A maintenance man huddles in the doorway of the snack pavilion and watches spirals of soil tube out of the earth and through the grass hidden, the snow, reaching a shovel as far as it will reach and pushes back the rising mounds. He scoops scoops of soil and tosses them back keeping back the encroaching crust. Trees uproot. Buildings tremble.

The End Times, The Extreme Sizzler, The Famine, The Financial Crisis, The Fire Brigade, The Flies, The Gargantua, The Gyroscope, The Home Wrecker,

A phone rings in the room next door. The television goes gray and then white. He lights a red candle and inhales the cinnamon smoke. Something trembles. They are lovers long transformed. He stands at the foot of the bed. Winter beats against the outside walls. A shingle peels away from the roof and flaps in the wind. Clouds vibrate. The sky vibrates. They can no longer speak.

The Hurricane, The Locusts, The Long Death, The Lovemaker, The Mauler, The Molester, The

A jogger sinks ankle deep in bubbling mud and pulls her feet from her shoes and

Murderer, The Octopus, The Other War, The Prom Date, The Riv

A maintenance man huddles

His watch falls.

A woman on her way to work falls

A woman breaks her ankle

er of Blood, The Ruiner, The Scrambler, The Sizzler,
Space Mountai
n, The Spinout, The Spouse, The Tidal
Wave, The Tornado, The Twin Towe
rs, The Twister, The Typhoon, The Wagon Wheel, The W
ar, The Wipe-Out, The Y
o-Yo.

A woman on her way to work
A man
A woman a small world,   A   Teacup,   Broken   ,
Century   , The   , The   , The End   , The
End   , The Exploder, The   Sizzler, The   , The
Fi   r   , e Fire   , The F i ,   r   , e Gyr   e,
The   Wreck , The

He tries to find his watch.
He stands at the foot of the bed. He trembles. He crawls
across the bed and straddles her. He reaches to lift the sunglasses from her face but she stops him.

  , The   , The Locus , The Lo   , The Love   , The   , The M
,   aker, The O   , The   Wa ,   r Da ,   nger,
The River   , The Ruin , The S   ,   S   ,
    The Sky   ,   Mountai
    n, The Sp   , The Spouse, The   ,
    The T   , The T   T
    , The T   , The T   , The   Wheel, The W
    ar, The W   Out, The Y
    o-Yo.

———

"Leave the sunglasses," she says. They are transformed.

A man walking a dog huddles in the door of the pavilion.

A woman on her way to work is knee deep in waves of water and ice.

A maintenance man barricades himself in a doorway and fights the soil.

A raptor huddles in its cage hoisted high above and eats its own long frozen eggs cracking each shell with beak tip, sucking the thick, cold yoke. One it swallows whole and one rolls from the nest and falls through the cage wires and falls through trees and wires, falling, shattering on the hard ground. Each day the raptor lays new eggs and eats them.

A tidal wave erupts miles away, miles of hands reaching toward the sky.

Miles of light.

The locus, the lovers, the makers, the war, the river, the ruins. The Sky. Mountain.

"We should   ," he says. "We should have   last ."

A maintenance man huddles in the doorway of the pavilion. Soil   out of the earth in spirals. Through the hidden grass, through the snow. He reaches

          pushes back the rising mounds. He tosses soil back, keeping back the encroaching crust.

Antennas bend and break. Satellites explode fireworks in the sky. Invisible bodies, invisible disasters.

She nods. He hovers   her and   her eyes.

He lowers   and   is so close he can feel the warmth of her breath. His thin arms tremble. She folds her body from beneath him and reaches for

I have my own stupid mouth to the blood vessels
As the spring in the mountains of the same mouth absorbs

     hoisted   and eats its own
cracking
     , sucking   . One it swallows
     and wires,
falling, shattering on   .   eats
them.

He falls across   bent   .
The lips   *in the spring*   ;
Love and gather   *drips and fall and*
     injury.

She covers her   .
     She cannot
     this.
And I tell
     the air
How long   *heavenly stars*
His thin arms tremble. His arms tremble. He   .
The ground swallows   . The ground   new ground and eats   ground.

Iceland

Radiates darkness, and light without heat, the island
  a cave turned outward. Climbing stairs to find the source of
all water falls, climbing just one more hill looking for a view of
some dirty glacier, cold skin peeling from the white sky.
  Only moss grows wild. Show me
  the palms of your hands,
  show me your fingers, show me
  what moves below your skin, please,
  because we have been walking these soft green paths all day
and it will never be night and even without trees it is as if shade
constantly covers us.
  Show me the hair on
  your arms moving in the wind and I will show you
  Show me cold water flowing and

Some Kirkpatricks

Over 500,000 people die in major Russian cities, the Philippines, and the Ottoman Empire during the sixth cholera pandemic.

The inhalation of vaporized mercury is believed to be an effective treatment for syphilis.

Pineapples, potatoes, and radishes are known to cure warts.

Polio transmission is primarily oral-faecal.

Legionnaires' disease was not called Legionnaires' disease until an outbreak in 1976 infects attendees at an American Legion Meeting in Philadelphia, PA, leading to the discovery of a new strain of bacterium, named *Legionella* for the first identifiable carriers of Legionnaires' disease. Legionnaires' disease is named in honor of the Legionnaires who bravely contracted Legionnaires' disease.

The mercury cure works by killing the patient.

Kirkpatrick leaves his mortal life on August 13, 1920. He is survived by his beloved wife, two sisters, two sons. He is preceded in death by his mother and father. Though it is believed that his soul was smaller than average, he is a beloved father and will be remembered for his kind smile and experiments with potatoes.

A small soul can slide through the gates of heaven, undetected.

The victims of flood, but not the Great Flood of 1889. The family of Kirkpatrick leaves their mortal lives on September

1, 1905, their modest valley home devastated by cascading rain and thick walls of mud converging on them while they sleep. Had they only heard the heavy wings of ascending crows warbling through the thick flood air.

Crows taking flight at night are flood harbingers.

Wasting is the process by which we waste. Muscle and fat tissue melt together. Skin slackens. Stunting is acute. Starvation. Chronic Wasting is a transmissible spongiform encephalopathy, caused by prions and is found primarily in cervids.

Tuberculosis is vampirism.

Typhoid. Symptoms: Malaise. Rose-red chest.

In the cold night. Stars burning through darkness.

Thick black blood down the canal of skin above the lips.

Kirkpatrick left his mortal life on October 31, 1857. Survived by a daughter, a son, a wife. Preceded in death by a mother and a father. Suffered from arc-eye staring too long at the sun. Fell from his bicycle and hit his head.

Approximately 16 million people died in the Great War.

Two thousand two hundred and nine people died in the

Great Flood. The Hurricane of 1900 killed between 6,000 and 12,000 people.

Fuch's dystrophy starts in the morning when the eye clouds.

House Finch Eye Disease kills millions of birds in North America.

Crows implicated: gastroenteritis, avian cholera, Histoplasma capsulatum spores, flooding. Onions protect against crows.

Apoplectic. Died from stroke. Died from a small hole burning through his heart.

Unknown causes.

Scroffula can be cured by the touch of the King of England.

Effluviatic.

Invented and patented a device for mimicking the sound of croaking bullfrogs in order to ease the onset of sleep. Leaves behind a family, a Great Dane, a fragment of a red wool scarf knitted by his mother for his fifth birthday tucked beneath blankets in the cedar chest at the foot of the bed.

Broken bones mended by amputation.

Body badly burned.

Survivors survive.

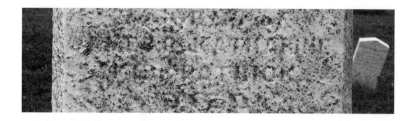

Passed away at home. Born. A member. Blessed. Will be missed. Is survived by. Preceded in death. Funeral services will be held. The family will receive friends.

Weight discrepancy: 33 pounds, 5 ounces.

Birth discrepancy: 123 days.

Height discrepancy: 4.3 inches.

Age discrepancy at death: 6514 days.

Difference of soul weight: .45 ounces (estimated).

Kirkpatrick alone for 17 years, 10 months, 1 day. Kept track for 1 year, 3 months, 2 days. Never remarried.

Vertical distance between bodies: 2.5 feet (approximate).

Minor differentiators: emotional capacity, short-term memory, appetite, favorite child.

Kirkpatrick, a survivor of the Fifth Cholera Epidemic.
Succumbs to heart disease in 1937.

August 5, 1937: The Soviet Union begins the Great Purge,
purging 724,000 (approximate) anti-Soviet elements.

August 18, 1937, Kirkpatrick notices minor influenza
symptoms and postpones a visit with her sister to the Great
Salt Lake.

On September 2, 1937, 11,000 (approximate) die in the Great
Hong Kong Typhoon.

At age 75, Kirkpatrick is hit by an ice-cream truck walking from her parked car, a blue 1949 Dodge Coronet, toward
Woolworth's to buy a new winter coat. Survived by daughters,
a son, granddaughters, and a grandson who agrees to take care
of Kirkpatrick's parakeet, Lester, and Dachshunds, Lippy and
Dashell.

Kirkpatrick ordained December 17, 1944. U.S. Army Chap-
lain. Veteran. Poor cook.

Lazy eye. Visited Niagara Falls three times.

Dies winding his watch.

Experiences symptoms: dizziness, sensation of fullness in chest, sweating, shortness of breath, indigestion.

Kirkpatrick awakens late in the morning on October 19, 1975. A strong wind rattles the windows. Stands shirtless on the edge of the front porch watching dust twist through the air. A rusty bicycle rests against a maple tree. A fallen branch scrapes along the road, blown by the steady wind, warm for October. He touches his left elbow with his right hand and rubs raw the dry skin. A cat sleeps beneath a parked car. Three potted chrysanthemums wilt unwatered on the concrete walk. A crow watches from a fork formed by thick tree branches.

Forty-three die in the Moorgate tube crash on February 28, 1975, in London, England. Forty-six die during the October 6, 1976, Massacre in Bangkok, Thailand.

Kirkpatrick dies in her sleep March 14, 1950.

March 17: discovery of element 98. On November 1, 1952, element 98, californium, along with plutonium and einsteinium, observed in the fallout from the first U.S. test of the hydrogen bomb.

January 12: 64 killed in collision between British submarine *Tuculent* and a Swedish oil tanker.

February 1, 1974, fire in São Paulo kills 177 and later 11.

February 17, 1974, soccer in Cairo kills 49.

April 3, 1974, 149 tornadoes kill 315.

September 8, 1974, a bomb in an airplane causes the airplane to crash into the Ionian Sea, killing 88.

September 9, 1974: a violent storm, Kirkpatrick alone, Kirkpatrick having died three years prior, the victim of unsolved violence. The lights light then dark then light again and again. A crow calls. Stumbling through the kitchen looking for the candle on the kitchen counter. Knocks over a pitcher full of

thin lemonade, fresh that afternoon. The pitcher falls from the counter and shatters, glass shards beneath bare foot-falls. Falls against counter and hits head on the edge. Slips onto the floor and fades, broken glass pushing into Kirkpatrick's cheeks. Behind the stove a mouse begins to eat a mouse dead in a trap.

Kirkpatrick dies. Kirkpatrick is born. Kirkpatrick dies.

Kirkpatrick opens the lock shop lock and carts the items on sale out onto the sidewalk still wet from early rain. The smell of smoke drifting from a barrel fire deep in an alley two blocks away stains the morning air. The power lines above sag beneath the weight of crows. The cracks in the sidewalk slowly widen. Kirkpatrick arranges locks, boxes, and chains on the table and again inside he turns on the lights and begins to dust. Kirkpatrick opens the cash register. Closes it. Rings the bell hanging above the door to hear it ring. Begins to unlock and lock the rows of locks hanging from the wall on hooks. Wraps his index finger in a cloth, unlocks each box, and moves his finger to clean each dark corner. A woman wrapped in blankets wanders in and out. Kirkpatrick follows her to the street where she shivers. Thick, wet blisters pock her neck. Even though it is not cold, it is not warm. She walks toward the slow smoke, still ribboning through the air. Kirkpatrick fingers the wine cork he carries in his right pants pocket. Kirkpatrick checks the time on his watch and winds it. It had been his son's watch.

After a day in the empty store, after the soot rises from the railroad shop smokestacks fingering the sky to cover the sun, after Kirkpatrick has closed the door and locked every lock, he will walk the filthy street toward the new Model B he will borrow from Kirkpatrick who has hidden a keg of beer in the back of the car beneath a horse hair blanket. He will drive away from the dusk of downtown, rumbling through yellow fields into the hills where he will turn down a gravel road almost too narrow for the car until he comes to a baseball field hidden in the hills among trees beneath a bluer sky. Kirkpatrick will help Kirkpatrick roll the keg to the improvised seats and the crowd will crowd around them holding their steins and wait for a drink. They will listen to the crack of a baseball hit long into the woods.

Late, after darkness has ended the game, after the keg has emptied, Kirkpatrick will drive Kirkpatrick down the road, meandering down the hill and back into city. They'll pass the murky light of the railroad shops, the rolling mill, an empty coal train, a mile long, waiting to go into the mountains. They will make a stop at a white-turned-gray row house, walk around back to the cellar door and in the basement bar, have another round. Kirkpatrick will drive Kirkpatrick home on back roads.

Kirkpatrick will die quietly sleeping, the sky clear and black and cold for the first time in months.

Kirkpatrick will die sleeping, the sky cold and clear and black. A memory of.

Kirkpatrick felt the stone in his shoe intermittently as not a sharp pain, but something dull like a thumb pressing into the arch of his foot. He shook his foot as he walked to jostle the stone into some safe place in his shoe, not wanting to stop and be caught in the rain. He ran across the street, the headlamps of a car emerging through the thick rain.

Walking home beyond dusk. Arms heavy with groceries. The second hottest summer on record. She can feel the grocery bags slipping from her arms, stops to adjust them back into the proper position. A dog barks from behind a fence. Kirkpatrick walks on the gravel sidewalk up the long, steep slope toward her home. She takes the short cut, a long concrete staircase overgrown with vines bisecting two long-empty lots.

She hears something crawling through the growth and stops to adjust her bags and catch her breath. She feels the cold sweat on her back. With twenty-two steps to go she stands and checks the grocery bags to make sure they won't break and continues. A bird calls to her from the thin bare branch of a dead and dry oak. At the top of the stairs, a block from home, she can smell the smoke of her neighbor's grill. When she gets home she'll take a glass of water onto the back porch and say hello and ask them what they're cooking. They'll offer her some of the chicken they're grilling and she'll thank them, because it's much too hot to cook. Kirkpatrick will sit in the green glider beneath the awning and she'll smile at the children laughing and shouting, running in circles in the shade of the neighbor's back lawn as the sun begins to set.

She'll go to bed early, exhausted from the heat, and as she falls asleep she will wonder if the she's put the milk away or left it on the counter and decides that if she's forgotten, it's too late.

One last drink. One more dance before a sobering walk around the block.

A knife across the throat. Trachea, esophagus lacerated.

Pneumonia, influenza, tuberculosis.

A day after another day. Kirkpatrick up in bed, in darkness, something tapping against the window. Something fluttering against the inside of his chest. Some pain boring out of him, pushing against his sternum, trying to escape. Something strangling his lungs. Short, quick breaths. Kirkpatrick beside him something like sleep and at the same time not sleep. Survived by Kirkpatrick. Kirkpatrick a year to the day later, in bed on the quietest night, alone.

A reactor explodes. An airplane crashes. A dam breaks. A train derails.

A bacterial infection, a bacterial meningitis. Syphilitic complication. Head pain, fever, fear of light. Fear of darkness. A dusting of snow. Thin, invisible ice. A power line, down. A seizure. A deer, dead, frozen in the road.

Survived by a sixteen-acre apple orchard. Survived by an herb garden long succumbed to mint. Survived by an empty doghouse rotting.

Survived by: a dull kitchen knife in the kitchen sink, the residue of a solitary dinner, a plate on the end-table, the blue light of the television, the dust-covered drapes, a clear vinyl path through the living room to the bedroom over the pristine white carpet, a collection of miniscule glass animals, grass unmowed, a rhubarb patch, untended, a five gallon bucket full of broken glass, a red car in a white garage, asphalt in need of patching, seventeen hidden Bibles: beneath the sink, beneath the pillow, beneath the couch cushion, on the nightstand, between the towels, beneath the driver's seat, beneath the *TV Guide*, behind the microwave, in the oven beneath bags of pretzels, in the coffee table drawer, on the second attic step, beneath a coffee can full of nails on a shelf in the garage, in the freezer, in the crisper, in a twenty-pound bag of rice, on a shelf in the basement below a box of fuses, beneath the family album, well worn and marked, photographs of Kirkpatrick and Kirkpatrick and Kirkpatrick brittle and torn, so thick the bible binding has broken, the leather cover hanging by the end-papers.

Encephalitis lethargica kills millions between 1917 and 1928.

Cholera. Influenza. Black Death. Plague. Plague. Smallpox. Fever. Malaria. Foot and Mouth Disease. Plague. Cholera. Influenza. Ebola. Infantile Paralysis. Typhus. Plague. Smallpox. Mumps. HIV.

Swine Flu. Infects humans and pigs, but never birds. Affects the cloven-hoofed. Elephants susceptible, as are hedgehogs. Incubates for 2–12 days. High fever. Oral blisters. Drooling.

Inflamed heart sometimes leads to explosion.

A frayed power cord from the toaster oven to the outlet in the wall.

An abandoned nest of crows in the chimney.

Six drafty rooms.

A brown recluse in the overgrown garden.

Rhinovirus, salmonella, Escherichia coli, Staphylococcus aureus, Yersinia, pestis.

Cryptosporidium muris: refrigerator handle, stove handle, door handles, bread box, salt and pepper shakers, light switches, broomstick, telephone, bathroom faucet, kitchen tile, kitchen counter, television dials, lamp switch, *TV Guide.*

Kirkpatrick aged 74 years, 7 months, and 20 days. Beloved Mother, friend, and lover. Passed away. Peacefully passed. Left this life. Left this presence. Returned to heaven. Left this world. Embraced family. Loved by her family. Loving mother and grandmother. Lived righteously. Charitable. Active. Outgoing. Retired. Worked. Lived. Dedicated. Educated. Survived. Suffered complications.

A viewing will be held. Services will be held. Condolences may be sent.

Kirkpatrick could not remember being born and will not remember dying, the last deep breath, the last short shrill inhalation, unsatisfied, wanting just one more, the lack of light or darkness, the feeling of the soul pounding against the inside of the ribcage desperately looking for some secret escape, the feeling of the thick hard pillow on the back of the skull, the tired, stiff neck, the feeling of being bedridden for three days that felt so long but were not long enough, the taste of broth and salt and something bland like potatoes or oatmeal, the feeling of swallowing, the feeling of water on the lips, the feeling of trying to sit up in bed, the feeling of fighting sleep as if every last noticed thing is something to savor, struggling to tell another story, the smell of Kirkpatrick like something withering, the feeling of overwhelming warmth, the sound of laughter in the kitchen downstairs, the smell of bacon in the morning and something roasting in the oven at night, the feel of a hand on her forehead, the feeling of fingers intertwining her own fingers, the feeling of a whisper on her earlobe, the sound of a crow calling outside the window, the sound of geese flying overhead, a blurred

V transforming in the gray sky, the sound of leaves shaking and falling from the tree, the window cracked, the smell of impending winter, the smell of cold, thirst, a vision, a memory, a moment when a little air in the lungs is no longer enough.

Between 62 and 78 million die in the Second World War. Between 30 and 60 million die during the Mongol Conquests. Between 10 and 100 million die during European conquests in the Americas. Nine hundred and thirteen die in the Jonestown Revolutionary Suicide.

In 1931, between 1 and 4 million die in floods in China. In 1887, between 900,000 and 2 million die during Yellow River floods in China.

Bhola cyclone. Indian Ocean earthquake. Roopkund hailstorm. European heat wave.

Mount Tambora volcanic eruption. Mount Vesuvius volcanic eruption.

Peshtigo wildfire. Halifax explosion. Cinema Rex fire. Courriéres mine disaster.

Japan Airlines Flight 123, Turkish Airlines Flight 981, American Airlines Flight 587.

MV *Doña Paz*, SS *Kiangya*, MV *Joola*, SS *Sultana*, RMS *Titanic, Toya Maru*.

Champawat tiger, Tsavo man-eaters, Leopard of Rudraprayag, Tigers of Chowgarh.

Queen of the Sea train disaster, Modane train disaster.

Approximately 12 billion dead.

Estimated number of souls in heaven: 144,000.

Kirkpatrick after four beers climbs onto the roof and bal-
ances a ladder in the crook of a maple tree in the backyard. He
wraps the electric chainsaw around his shoulder by the power
cord and steps onto a thick branch, tests the ladder, and begins
to climb. At the top of the ladder he looks across the lawn
and can see his neighbor, her long body naked in the window,
combing her hair, watching him. He will climb one more rung
of the ladder. He will start the chainsaw and chew threw a
thick branch, the chainsaw too small and clogged for the job.
He will look again into his neighbor's window and she will be
standing there, still, her breasts, her stomach and arms. He will
remember the way he stumbled over his words. The chainsaw
will jump and kick and the ladder will vibrate on the branch
and he will wrap the tangled power cord over his shoulder and
behind his neck to avoid slicing through it and he will again
wonder why he bought an electric chainsaw, why he bought
something so small, why he planted so many trees so close to
the house on such a small lot. He will not look up because he
knows she is there, still, watching him. He will feel the ladder
sliding, will feel his foot slipping, feel the cord draped around
his body tightening around his neck.

Vaccines: plague, cholera, diptheria, flu, hepatitides A and B, human papillomavirus, influenza, measles, mumps, polio, rotavirus, rubella, tetanus, tuberculosis, varicella, yellow fever.

Seal houses against birds and drafts.

Wash hands often.

Hold breath.

Ignore dogs.

Protect dreams from death and birth.

Exercise often and with vigor.

Do not touch the dead.

Eat vegetables. Protect the skin. Limit alcohol.

Prevent eye twitching.

Do not hold funerals on Fridays. Do not count cars.

Wear well-worn clothes.

Remove clocks and mirrors.

No photographs.

Do not eat in groups of three or thirteen.

Hang umbrellas carefully.

Rise early.

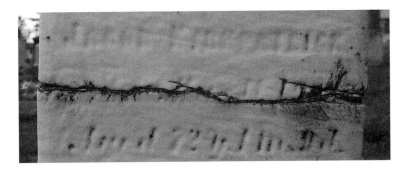

Avoid rats, snakes, turtles, butterflies, and all birds.

Violence, sickness, sleep: inevitable.

Kirkpatrick left his mortal life. Survived. Preceded. Suffered. Fissured. Died. Severe weakness, fever, abscess, pus, cankers, nausea.

Fluid accumulation, contortion, bleeding.

Disturbed functionality, hysteria, yellow eyes, yellow skin.

A bird in the house. A crow in the cupboard. A crow's gaze. Crow cawing. Crows. Robin through window.

A clock turning backward. A mirror shattering.

A barking dog. Open windows. Thunder indicates reckoning. Weeds grow over trapped souls. Parsley. Vultures. Seagulls in the number three. Roosters. Daylight owls. Banshees. Horse sounds. Dogs. Black dogs. Strange fish. Falling stars. Clouded water.

Stop clocks. Unlock locks. Unknot knots. Light one candle for every dead ancestor.

Heart stops beating. Lungs stop breathing. Blood no longer circulates.

Pale gray. Bruised, then blue.

Cells line up and die: brain, muscle, skin, bone.

Decay.

The soul escapes or fails to escape.

Bacteria eats the organs.

Enzymes exit the intestine and stomach and devour the body.

Cells consume cells.

Flies lay eggs in mouth, nose, ears, wounds.

Putrefy. Hydrogen sulfide, methane, cadaverine, putrescine.

Inflation. Insects.

The body blackens and liquefies. Mold.

The body dries. The soul's last chance.

Moth and bacteria.

The weight of all souls.

A name in stone eroding and bone.

Acknowledgments

Thank you to Susan McCarty, without whose love, encouragement, and inspiration, this book would not have been possible.

Thank you to my parents and my sisters, Alysa and Elena, for their love and support.

Thank you to all of my friends and colleagues at the University of Utah, especially my creative writing professors: Karen Brennan, François Camoin, Lance Olsen, and Melanie Thon; and the rest of my doctoral committee: Craig Dworkin, Joe Metz, and Kathryn Stockton. Thank you to my fellow graduate students who have provided friendship and inspiration: Neal Carroll, Kathryn Cowles, Shira Dentz, Barbara Duffey, Robert Glick, Andy Farnsworth, Stacy Kidd, Dawn Lonsinger, Rachel Marston, Cami Nelson, Tim O'Keefe, Jacob Paul, April Wilder, and all of the graduate students with whom I've shared classes, conversations, and good times.

Thank you to the members of Tent Preacher for the rock and roll: Geoffrey Babbitt, Missy Molloy, and Ely Shipley.

Thank you to friends, teachers, and writers who have offered advice and encouragement: Alexa Beattie, Matt Bell, Bill Black, Blake Butler, Todd Carter, Jason Cherkis, Mark Farrington, Jennifer Gendel, Lily Hoang, Dave Housley, Jeff Kaufman, Steve Kistulentz, Brian Kubarycz, Chris MacAulay, Alan Michael Parker, Richard Peabody, Davis Schneiderman, Gary Smith, Jeremy Trylch, Joe Warminsky, and the rest of the Barrelhouse crew: Dan Brady, Mike Ingram, Joe Killiany, Tom McAllister, and Aaron Pease.

Thank you to the FC2 Board of Directors, especially Matt Roberson; and Carmen Edington, Lou Robinson, Dan Waterman, and Tom Williams at FC2.

Thank you to the following journals in which some of these stories first appeared: *Action, Yes!; Center: A Journal of Literary Arts; Copper Nickel; The Collagist; Diagram; elimae; Gargoyle; Harp & Altar; Lamination Colony;* the *Notre Dame Review; Pank; Redivider; Web Conjunctions;* and *Western Humanities Review.*